Anchored in Hope

Echoes in Camano Island

Kimberly Thomas

Prologue

"I am so sorry for your loss, dear. Your mother was a phenomenal woman. The members of the bridge club miss her dearly."

"Thank you, Mrs. Lee. It means a lot that you came," Lacy's voice emerged in a soft murmur, gratitude lacing each syllable. Her face was a mask of perfected grace as her lips curved upward in response to the older woman's touch. The weight of her hand on Lacy's arm was another attempt at offering comfort amidst the sea of condolences and mournful whispers.

As the woman walked away, Lacy looked ahead at the line of cars pulling up and people exiting them, as they made their way up to the house to express their condolences. She inadvertently pulled in a sharp breath as she braced herself. All she wanted to do was curl up in her bed and cry herself to sleep, but it wasn't possible at the moment. At her mother's repast, she had to play the role of a perfect hostess, smiling while wanting to cry, returning words of gratitude when all she wanted to do was scream.

1

Feeling a presence beside her, she lifted her head to see her husband standing there, and automatically, a smile lifted her lips.

"Hey." Carlos smiled tenderly as his hand came up to rub her back lovingly. "How are you feeling?"

"I'm...trying," she softly confessed.

Carlos tilted his head in a subtle nod, his hazel eyes tracing hers as they flickered with compassionate understanding. "I'm here for you. We'll get through this... together," he said, repeating the words he had spoken so often to her ever since the moment they found out about her mother's stomach cancer.

"I know, sweetie." She smiled gratefully before Carlos's lips tenderly covered hers. Warmth spread through her at the tender gesture. At that moment, she could not have loved and appreciated her husband more than she did.

"Where are the children?" she asked, looking behind her into the hall.

"They're in the kitchen with Mom. David is eating a snack, and she's making a bottle for Maria," he informed her.

"Okay," Lacy breathed out in relief.

"Lacy."

Lacy turned to the woman standing before her with a sympathetic look on her face and glistening brown eyes. "Hi, Jean. I'm glad you could make it." She smiled appreciatively as she fell into the woman's hug.

"Martha was like a mother to me. There's no way I would have missed paying my respects," Jean murmured against her cheek. "How are you holding up?" she asked when they separated.

"Honestly, I'm feeling a mix of emotions right now—

mostly denial that she's gone—but I'm grateful for the support from everyone, especially my husband," she answered and looked up at Carlos. He returned her smile.

"Hi." Jean's voice broke through their moment, causing the pair to turn toward her once more. She held her hand out in greeting.

"Hello," Carlos replied, extending his hand to grasp hers with a friendly smile.

"Jean, this is my husband, Carlos," Lacy introduced them. "Jean and I grew up back in San Antonio before Mom moved us here to Santa Monica," she further explained.

"It's always nice to meet a friend of Lacy's." Carlos nodded.

Jean gave a tight lipped tiny smile before she and Lacy exchanged a glance with each other. It had been years since the two had spoken, and it would have probably continued if Lacy's mom hadn't died.

"I brought a casserole," Jean said before the pause became awkward.

"That's very thoughtful. Thank you." Lacy smiled.

"I just need to take it out of the car," Jean informed her.

Lacy nodded. "You can put it in the kitchen."

"Okay," Jean replied, turning to head to her car. She abruptly turned to face Lacy again. "I hope we can get some time to catch up." Her voice held hope.

"Okay," Lacy replied with a slight upturn of her lips.

"What's the story with her?" Carlos asked as soon as the woman was out of earshot.

Lacy stared at Jean's retreating back before responding. "Mom was her nanny for ten years," Lacy revealed. "We were very close all through elementary, but when we got to high school, our friendship changed," she continued with a slump of her shoulders as her mind flashed to the event that ended their close friendship.

"Friendships can be restored," Carlos said encouragingly, rubbing her arm.

Jean walked up just then with the casserole. "I'll just head inside now," she said sheepishly.

Lacy nodded and watched her walk down the hall toward the kitchen. "I guess they can." Her voice was laced with a hint of hesitancy.

"Lacy, dear." She turned just then to receive a hug from another of her mother's old bridge partners.

"Hi, Alice," she greeted.

The rest of the time went by in a blur, and as the last guest filed out of the house, Lacy sighed. Her shoulders had been stiff all day, deflated.

"Mom?"

"Yes, sweetheart?" Lacy returned, staring down at her seven-year-old son.

His innocent hazel eyes, so much like his father's, stared up at her with unasked questions. "Is Heaven real?"

Lacy sucked in a surprised breath. "Of course, it is real, sweetheart," she answered with a smile of reassurance.

"How do you know that Grandma is there?" David pressed, his voice filled with anguish.

"Well, Grandma lived her life loving people and being selfless. There's always a place up there for people like her."

"But what if that wasn't enough?" David pushed.

"I believe wherever she is, she's...happy and free from pain," Lacy answered, willing her lips to lift into a smile of reassurance. She wished he never had to think about questions like these at a young age and there was some way she could shield him from it all.

"I wish she didn't have to go. I...I miss her."

"I know you do. I do too." Lacy wiped the tears running down her son's cheek as she fought to keep her own tears at bay. "But she is in a better place now. Get some sleep; we can talk more about this in the morning." She leaned over him and planted a gentle kiss against his cheek before rising from the chair by his bedside and heading for the door.

"Mom?"

Lacy turned to her son.

"I love you," David called out.

"I love you too." Lacy smiled, then turned and exited the room. Her back slumped against his door as the tears she'd kept in all day burst through the barrier and cascaded down her face. She bit her lip to contain a sob as her heart ached.

"Hey," Carlos's tender voice startled her. Without hesitation, she flew into his waiting arms, the warmth from his body heating her. "Everything will be okay." He ran his hand over her hair soothingly as her tears soaked his shirt.

When her sobs had subsided, Carlos led her down the hall toward their room and helped her prepare for bed. "Maria's sleeping in the guest room with Mom," he informed her before she asked. Lacy nodded before getting under the covers he had pulled back for her. He got in on the other side before bundling her into his arms.

Lacy held tightly to the arm across her chest as she stared at the wall. A few minutes later, Carlos's rhythmic breathing against her neck told her he had fallen asleep, but she couldn't.

Her mind kept replaying her mother's last instructions to her before she had taken a turn for the worse. Her mother's frail yet resolute voice echoed in her head, "Read the letter, my love, after I'm gone."

She had been too wrought with grief then to heed her mother's last wish. But tonight, the silence was stifling, the void too vast. Slipping out from under Carlos's arm and out of the comfort of their bed, she walked to the closet, removed the small box where she kept her memorabilia, and took out the envelope. She then made her way to the bathroom and gently closed the door, not wanting to wake her husband.

Seated on the cool tile of the bathroom floor, her hands trembled as she opened the envelope and unfolded the neatly creased paper.

My dear Lacy...

The familiarity of those words brought both comfort and a pang of sorrow, reminding her that her mother's voice would forever be captured within the confines of this letter.

I am so sorry I had to leave you like this. But I am comforted to know your life is full of love and the support of Carlos and my beautiful grandbabies. If it were any different, I would not have been able to go. I have lived my life, and I have had many regrets. But you, my sweet, sweet girl, you are the greatest joy of my life...

Lacy's tears left wet splotches on the paper as her mother's words resonated.

I wanted to shield you from all the ugliness of this world, but I was selfish because, in doing so, I held back a part of who you are. It is only fair I explain what happened so many years ago. I met a young man I thought would change my life forever; only then I did not know how...

As she read, memories flooded her mind, vivid images from her childhood etched in her consciousness. And there it was, amidst the swirling tapestry of recollections, a snapshot of a moment she had played over in her mind on countless occasions. Lacy, a wide-eyed five-year-old, stood in the living room doorway, a silent witness to a tumultuous exchange that would shape her life in ways she could not comprehend.

In her memory, her mother and a man she did not know were engaged in a heated argument. The man's face contorted with anger; his voice laced with bitterness.

"I told you not to have the child," he spat, his words cutting through the air like shards of ice. *"I won't be a part of this, and I don't want you interfering with my life."*

But her mother, strong-willed and resolute, stood her ground. "Our child is a blessing," she insisted, her voice trembling with a mixture of defiance and vulnerability. *"I will do whatever it takes to give her a good life."*

"Well, that's on you. Have a good life, Martha."

"We will have a good life without you," her mother spat back.

The man walked away from the clash, but his steps faltered as his blue gaze fell upon young Lacy. His eyes locked with her for a fleeting moment, and his sharp features relaxed as he stared at her in wonder. But just as quickly, it disappeared, and his lips set in a harsh line as his eyes narrowed. He stared over his shoulder at her mother before he turned and walked past Lacy, vanishing from their lives.

Confusion and curiosity overwhelmed Lacy, her young

voice breaking the tense silence. "Who was that, Mommy?"
she asked, her innocence seeking answers.

Her mother, her face etched with sadness and regret,
mustered a weak smile. "Oh, sweetheart, that was no one
important," she replied, her voice tinged with a mixture of
protectiveness and sorrow.

As Lacy's eyes continued to scan the pages of the
letter, her tears mingled with the inked words, blurring
the lines that etched her mother's thoughts. She had
always sensed the truth, the unspoken secret woven into
the fabric of her existence, but had been too afraid to ask
her mother about it—too afraid to upset her. And now, in
her mother's final words, the truth was laid bare
before her.

As she reached the end of the letter, her mother's
voice echoed in her mind, reaffirming what she had
already known deep within her soul. The man who had
argued with her mother all those years ago was, indeed,
her father.

Your father's name was Stuart Murphy.

Chapter One

Lacy

"All right, guys, it's time to go!" Lacy shouted down the hall, her voice echoing in the emptiness of her Santa Monica home. The rooms that once held laughter and warmth now felt cold and hollow. She took a deep breath, her heart heavy with mixed emotions as she prepared to embark on a new chapter in her family's life.

Outside, the sun cast a golden hue on the neatly trimmed lawn where the moving truck sat, a stark reminder of the imminent departure. Boxes were neatly stacked, waiting to be transported to their new home on Camano Island. Lacy glanced at the piles of belongings, a tangible representation of the life they were leaving behind.

The clicking sound against the wooden floors caught her attention, and she turned her head to see her seventeen-year-old son dragging his suitcase behind him, his brows furrowed and his jaw clenched, revealing the simmering anger that consumed him. Her eleven-year-old followed closely behind him with her own suitcase, her eyes following her footsteps.

"I can't believe you're making us do this," David muttered, his voice tinged with anger.

Lacy released a steadying breath. "I know this is hard for you, David," she said softly, her voice tinged with understanding. "But we don't have another option. What we do have is a chance to start fresh. Camano Island will be different, but maybe it's what we need right now."

David's eyes bored into his mother's, a mixture of resentment and sadness swirling within them. "My friends are here. My life is here," he emphasized with his index finger pointing downward in defiance.

"David," Lacy breathed out, pinching the bridge of her nose. "We can't stay here."

"Fine. I'll go stay with Shane. His parents don't have a problem with me staying with them," he reasoned.

"That is not an option," Lacy refused.

"Why not? This was supposed to be my breakout year to score a swimming scholarship. I won't have a chance if I have to move to Camano Island," David countered.

"You're not staying in Santa Monica, and that is final," Lacy returned, her voice rising. Realizing her frustration was getting the better of her. She drew in a deep breath before slowly releasing it. She reached out to gently rest her hand on his shoulder. "I know it's difficult, honey, but this is our best option. Plus, the high school in Camano Island has a good swim team; based on what I've heard, I'm sure we'll be able to get you on it."

Anger clouded David's expression. "I didn't ask for any of this," he seethed before stomping away. Lacy watched helplessly as he opened the front door and stepped through it before slamming it. She turned then to see Maria quietly watching her with wide, alert eyes. The corners of her mouth turned downward in a subtle frown that revealed their unease.

"What do you think?" Lacy asked.

Maria simply shrugged her shoulders as her lips turned up slightly. Lacy's own lips twitched downward as she stared at her once vibrant daughter, who had become an introvert the last two years of her father's death. Her silence served as a shield against the pain that had engulfed their lives. Lacy's heart ached for her daughter.

Walking over to Maria, Lacy placed a hand on her shoulder in reassurance as she spoke, "I know it's hard on you too. But we're in this together. We'll find happiness again. I promise."

Maria nodded, her voice barely audible. "Okay, Mom." With renewed determination and the faintest glimmer of optimism, Lacy led her daughter out of the house, their suitcases trailing behind them.

Lacy loaded the suitcases into the car, making sure they were secure for the long journey ahead. As she closed the trunk, she took a final look at their now-empty house, bidding a bittersweet farewell to the memories they had shared within its walls.

Taking a deep breath, she turned to her children, her voice filled with determination. "Let's go." Without a word, David pulled on his shades and got into the back seat. Maria got in after him.

Lacy got into the driver's seat, slowly the car pulled away from the curb and away from the house she had spent the last eighteen years in. Her heart weighed heavy as she steered the car along the seemingly endless road, the miles stretching out before her like an uncharted territory. The California sun blazed high in the sky, casting a golden hue over the landscape. The road snaked through rolling hills, adorned with swaying grasses and occasional clusters of wildflowers that painted the countryside with bursts of vibrant colors.

After hours of driving, Lacy decided it was time for a much-needed break. "Why don't you stop for a bit? Who's hungry?" She looked at her kids through the rearview mirror.

"I am," Maria answered softly.

David's shades and the fact he had in his headphones covering his ears made it hard for Lacy to determine whether he had heard her or if he was asleep. She turned her attention back to the road.

Five minutes later, spotting an IHOP nestled on the outskirts of Fresno, she guided the car into the parking lot, bringing it to a halt. The scent of freshly brewed coffee and warm pancakes wafted through the air and beckoned. Lacy stepped out of the car, as did Maria.

"Sweetie, can you ask your brother if he's coming?" Lacy smiled encouragingly at her daughter.

Maria's brown eyes filled with hesitation, but she nodded and walked over to David's side of the car.

"What?" Lacy heard her son's grumpy voice. She didn't hear what Maria said to her brother, but she heard him release a loud sigh before pushing the door open and stepping out of the car.

David walked past Lacy, the shades still covering his eyes, but his headphones were now hanging from his neck.

Lacy shook her head, exasperated, as she and Maria walked after him toward the restaurant.

The familiar aroma of sizzling bacon and a sizzling

griddle greeted them, mingling with the chatter of patrons and the clinking of silverware; the restaurant was abuzz with activity.

"Hi, welcome to IHOP. What can I get you, lovely folks?" the waitress, a friendly middle-aged woman with a warm smile, asked.

"Hi. Can I have the steakburger with fries and a chocolate milkshake?" Lacy ordered.

"Sure thing," the woman replied, her smile never wavering. "And what can I get you two?" She turned her attention to Lacy's children.

"Can I have a burger and fries and a strawberry milkshake?" Maria asked, her voice barely above a whisper.

"Of course, sweetheart," the woman smiled encouragingly. "And for you?" she asked David.

David browsed the menu, taking his time. Lacy opened her mouth to say something when he spoke. "I guess I'll have the same as they're having and a caramel frappé," he ordered and put his headphones back on.

Lacy gave the woman an apologetic look.

"I'll have your order ready in no time," the woman chirped, not missing a beat.

As soon as the woman walked away, Lacy reached over and pulled down David's headphones.

"What?" he asked, eyes dancing with confusion.

"That was incredibly rude of you just now," Lacy said, getting straight to the point.

"What did I do?" David feigned innocence.

"David Carlos Lopez, don't you sit there and pretend you didn't just act rude to our server. I get that you're angry about moving, but that doesn't give you the right to act this way to someone you don't know and who has probably had a hard day serving others so far," Lacy chided.

"I didn't...I..." David stammered before lowering his gaze and the corners of his mouth curling downward. "Sorry," he finally muttered.

"Can I go use the restroom, please?" Maria's soft voice cut through the tension that had covered their booth.

"Okay, sweetie," Lacy turned and smiled encouragingly at her daughter. "I'll go with you." They slid out of the booth and headed for the bathroom.

Inside the brightly lit room, Maria hurriedly entered one of the stalls, her small frame disappearing behind the closed door. Lacy sighed softly; her gaze drawn to the long mirror that stretched across the wall above the row of sinks. Stepping closer, she studied her reflection, her tired eyes tracing the lines etched on her face.

Her once vibrant caramel-blond hair now cascaded wearily around her shoulders, strands losing their luster and vitality. Her fingertips brushed against the slight bags beneath her dark-brown eyes. The paleness of her skin was a stark contrast to its usual warm hue. Her heart ached as she glimpsed the toll that life had taken on her, her inner strength barely hanging on.

Turning on the faucet, she splashed some cold water over her face, trying to rejuvenate herself. Maria exited the stall then.

"Ready to go?" Lacy asked after Maria finished washing her hands.

Maria simply nodded. By the time they got back to David, their server was already depositing their food on the table.

"Here you go." She smiled after putting down the last milkshake.

"Thank you so much." Lacy smiled gratefully before nudging David under the table with her leg. He looked up, his expression a mix between annoyance and embarrassment.

"Yeah. Thanks for this." He turned to the server. His lips attempted a smile, but it looked more like a grimace.

"It was my pleasure." The woman smiled broadly. "Enjoy your meal now," she finished before walking off to serve another booth. Without another word, the trio dove into their sizzling burgers and crispy fries.

"We'll need to stop by a convenience store when we get back on the road. There are a few things I need to get before we get to Camano Island," Lacy informed her children. Glancing at David, she noticed his gaze was fixed on the plate before him, his jaw clenched tight. A soft sigh slipped through her lips. Thirty minutes later, they were back on the road.

As the last vestiges of a scarlet sunset faded into the twilight, Lacy's Subaru Exiga station wagon pulled into a small motel nestled on the outskirts. The neon sign buzzed intermittently, fighting against the encroaching darkness.

"Brrr. It's a bit chillier than I anticipated." Lacy shivered as her hands came up to rub her bare arms. Her breath formed a delicate cloud of vapor that danced before her face. Maria's little arms puckered with goosebumps as her teeth clanged against each other. The contrast between Santa Monica's balmy evenings and the biting Oregon chill was painfully evident.

Shivering, they hurriedly made their way toward the motel. On the other hand, David took his time walking after them, his hands in the pockets of his hoodie.

Entering the lobby, Lacy approached the reception

desk and greeted the man behind it. "Hi, can I have a room with two beds?"

The man glanced up from the comic book he was reading with a bored expression. He sighed heavily before rising to his feet without a word and retrieving a set of keys from the hook. "All rooms come with a queen-sized bed, but there is a sofa bed if you're looking for more space," he informed her in a monotonous drawl.

"Thanks," Lacy replied, handing him her ID and taking the keys.

"How long will you be staying, and will you be paying with cash or card?" the man asked while writing down her details.

"Um, just for the night and cash," she informed him.

"That'll be one hundred and forty-five dollars."

Digging in her purse, Lacy handed him the money.

"The room is the second door to your right on the first floor," the man informed her as he returned her ID. Giving him a half-crooked smile, she and her children made their way up the stairs.

Lacy cautiously stepped into their room, her eyes scanning the surroundings. Her face scrunched up in disappointment. Although the room appeared relatively clean, the signs of neglect and age were evident from the wallpaper peeling at the edges to the dull, outdated drapery blocking the windows and the bedspread with faded floral patterns clashing with the worn-out carpet beneath.

"Well, isn't this room just full of sunshine," David muttered, his tone dripping with sarcasm. He carefully tossed his knapsack onto the sofa bed before flopping beside it.

"It's only for one night," Lacy reminded him, her voice tinged with weariness.

"Yeah, and then it's back on the road to go live in some godforsaken town," he retorted bitterly.

"David," Lacy sighed. "Can you just not tonight?" she pleaded, her tired eyes searching his face for a glimmer of understanding.

"Yeah, whatever," David grumbled, his voice laced with indifference. With a swift motion, he retrieved his headphones and slipped them over his ears as his eyes slammed shut.

Lacy stared at him for a long time before softening her expression and turning to Maria. "Why don't you go get ready for bed? I'm sure you must be tired after such a long day," she encouraged.

"Okay," Maria answered with a slight tilt of her lips before heading to the bathroom.

Late into the night, after her children had fallen asleep, Lacy lay staring unseeingly into the ceiling as the weight of their situation threatened to crush her. She wished her children would understand the sacrifices she's had to make to ensure they were okay. It had been hard to move forward after Carlos's death two years ago, especially with the looming medical bills, the mortgage, and her maxed-out credit cards. The final straw had been the notice of foreclosure on their home. She made a decision then—one that would keep her family together and ensure that they were okay.

"Oh, Carlos," she whispered to the heavens, "I miss you so much. I wish you were here...you'd know what to do.

Chapter Two

Lacy

Seattle unfolded before Lacy like an open book as the last bend in the highway revealed the city skyline. The setting sun painted the city in warm hues, the skyscrapers shimmering with a golden gleam against a backdrop of the sapphire-blue ocean. The Space Needle, a silver spear piercing the sky, stood proud and tall amidst the architectural marvels. Lacy's heart pounded in her chest; she was finally here.

Lacy glanced in the rearview mirror. David, with his perpetually furrowed brow and crossed arms, looked out the window with a mixture of annoyance, but there was also intrigue. The cityscape had managed to capture his attention, despite his grumpy demeanor. Maria, on the other hand, sat quietly beside her brother, her wide eyes taking in the sight with a sense of wonderment.

A while later, they pulled up outside a sleek glass building, the name "Lynch & Associates" emblazoned at the entrance.

Taking a deep breath, she spoke. "All right, guys, I need to get something from the lawyer and then we can be on our way. Let's go."

"Do we have to go in with you?" David asked pointedly.

"Yes," Lacy spoke with finality, leaving no room for discussion.

With a heavy sigh, he exited the car, followed by Maria. The trio then entered the building. The atmosphere inside was somber, adorned with dark wood furniture and framed photographs of landscapes. Lacy couldn't help but feel a shiver down her spine as they approached the reception desk.

"Hello, my name is Lacy Lopez. I have an appointment with Mr. Lynch," Lacy said to the receptionist, her voice betraying a mix of nervousness and anticipation.

The receptionist smiled politely. "Of course, Mrs. Lopez. Please have a seat. Mr. Lynch will be with you shortly."

They found a couple of empty chairs and settled down, waiting anxiously. Lacy's mind raced with questions about her estranged father and what the lawyer, whom she'd spoken to a total of five times in ten years, would have for her.

Finally, the door to Mr. Lynch's office swung open with a creak, revealing a dimly lit room adorned with mahogany furniture and shelves lined with leather-bound books. Lacy's eyes widened as she took in the scene, her heart beating like a drum in her chest. She watched intently as a middle-aged man with graying hair emerged from the darkness, his presence commanding and his demeanor exuding an air of professionalism. Mr. Lynch, dressed impeccably in a well-tailored suit, stepped forward, extending his hand in a gesture of greeting.

"Mrs. Lopez, I presume?" he inquired, his voice carrying a sense of authority. "I'm Frank Lynch, I was Stuart's attorney. I'm glad you reconsidered."

Lacy, her mind swirling with a mix of apprehension and anticipation, rose from her seat, her hands trembling ever so slightly. She approached Mr. Lynch, her gaze locked with his, and tentatively clasped his outstretched hand. A nervous chuckle escaped her lips, betraying the unease that pulsed through her veins.

"Well, it's been ten years," she began, her voice wavering. "I thought, why wait another ten more for retribution from a father who wasn't in my life?" Her attempt at levity was met with a sympathetic look from the lawyer, his eyes filled with understanding.

Mr. Lynch, his face etched with a mix of empathy and professionalism, motioned toward the open door leading to his office. "Why don't we go into my office? We have quite a bit to discuss," he suggested, his tone gentle yet firm.

Lacy nodded, her mind racing with a million thoughts and emotions. With a deep breath, she followed Mr. Lynch into the sanctum of his office. Her eyes were immediately drawn to the centerpiece of the room, a massive desk crafted from rich, dark wood. Stacks of papers, meticulously arranged, adorned its surface, hinting at the weighty matters that awaited their attention. The room exuded an aura of gravitas as if every decision made within these walls carried consequences that rippled through lives and destinies.

She shifted nervously in her seat, her fingers tapping against the armrest. The weight of her decision pressed heavily on her mind. She had spent her entire childhood and adult life unaware of her father's existence and had only learned of his passing from a letter her deceased mother had left her as a parting gift. She hadn't wanted to find out about him or anything remotely related to him. So, when Mr. Lynch finally contacted her nine years ago to inform her of her inheritance—a house—she made it clear she had no interest in it. However, circumstances had now forced her hand, leaving her with no choice but to accept.

Mr. Lynch slid a stack of papers toward her. "These are just some formalities, nothing to worry about," he assured her as she signed where he pointed. Next, he presented her with a set of keys. "As you are aware, Stuart left you a house on Camano Island," he spoke matter-of-factly.

Mr. Lynch cleared his throat and handed her an envelope, his expression somber. "He also left this... this is a letter for you."

With trembling hands, Lacy opened the envelope. Scrawling handwriting filled the page. Lacy took a deep breath and began to read it softly.

My dear Lacy,

If you're reading this, it means I'm no longer a part of this world, leaving behind a trail of unanswered questions and unresolved emotions. I write to you now with a mixture of remorse and longing, to beg for your forgiveness and to shed light on the circumstances that shaped our fractured relationship.

I want to apologize for the pain I caused your mother all those years ago by my actions. I regret not being there for her, for you, and to not being able to watch you grow up. The last time I saw you, you were but a child, small and innocent. I wish I had done better. The decisions I made were driven by a desperate desire to protect the family I already had—a family that included your two half sisters. In my misguided pursuit of this perceived protection, I made grave errors that had far-reaching consequences. I failed all of you, succumbing to the weight of my own shortcomings as a father. If only I had possessed the foresight to see beyond my own fears and prioritize the love and connection you deserved.

In an attempt to make amends, I have entrusted a key to a woman named Nelly. She is an individual whom I trust implicitly, and I believe she will ensure that this key finds its way into your hands. To establish contact with her, please seek the assistance of Mr. Lynch, who will provide you with the necessary information.

Lacy, my words cannot fully encapsulate the depth of regret I feel for the years lost and the pain I have caused. I humbly beseech you to find it in your heart to forgive me, though I understand that forgiveness is a journey that may take time and healing. It is my fervent hope, through the passage of time, you will come to understand that even in my absence, my love for you has never waned. You have always held a cherished place within the recesses of my soul.

With profound remorse and unwavering love,
Stuart

Lacy's eyes filled with tears as she folded the letter back into the envelope. She had a lot to take in—a new town, a new house, a father's apology from beyond the grave, and a mysterious key.

"Here you go," Mr. Lynch handed her some tissues.

"Thank you," she managed to say, looking at the man through the tears blurring her vision. "I...I'm not usually like this, but this letter and everything that's been happening in my life...it's just... it's just a lot to take in," she confessed, her voice trembling with a mixture of confusion and sadness.

"That's okay, Mrs. Lopez. There is no judgment here," Mr. Lynch assured her, his expression radiating empathy. Lacy nodded as she dabbed the tears at the corners of her eyes.

When she'd finally calmed down, she asked, "In my fath—Stuart's letter, he mentioned I have two sisters. Do you know anything about them?"

Mr. Lynch's eyes softened, and he sighed gently. "I understand your curiosity," he said, his voice filled with quiet understanding, "but it's not my place to delve into that matter. Especially since I cannot say for certain if your sisters are aware of your existence."

Lacy's disappointment was palpable as she rocked her head back and forth. "Okay. I understand, Mr. Lynch. Thank you for your honesty," Lacy replied, her voice tinged with a touch of sadness. She gathered her composure, realizing she had to accept the limitations of what she could uncover in her father's absence. A silence settled over the room, punctuated only by the old grandfather clock in the corner.

"I wish there was more I could do to help ease some of the confusion you're having," Mr. Lynch expressed, as if reading her thoughts.

Lacy managed a reassuring smile. "That's okay. I understand."

With a final exchange of pleasantries, Lacy left Mr. Lynch's office, her heart heavy with unanswered questions, a signed copy of the title to the house in Camano Island, and a name, Nelly. The sun hung low in the sky, but the air was chilly as she stepped out onto the bustling Seattle streets.

"Do you guys want to grab lunch before we get back on the road?" she turned to ask her children.

"Yeah. Whatever," David replied in a disinterested tone.

"Yes," Maria replied.

Lacy nodded. "I saw a diner about two blocks away. Let's try that," she suggested. Maria fell into step with her, while David lingered behind as they made their way toward the establishment. Ten minutes later, they were seated in a booth in the diner, digging into their order, conversation at a minimum. Half an hour later, they were back on the road, making the hour-long journey to Camano Island.

Lacy watched as the urban landscape gradually gave way to more natural surroundings. Tall buildings were replaced by trees and open fields. The air shifted, growing fresher and crisper with each passing mile.

As the car meandered along the winding road that led to Camano Island, Lacy's excitement swelled within her, mirroring the anticipation building in her chest. She couldn't help but steal glances at the scenery unfolding before her, her eyes widening with wonder.

The road was flanked by majestic evergreen trees, their tall trunks standing as sentinels of nature's grandeur. Their branches swayed gracefully in the gentle breeze, casting playful shadows on the asphalt. Lacy could almost hear the rustle of leaves, a symphony of whispers that welcomed her to this new chapter of her life.

The fragrance of pine permeated the air, its sweet scent mingling with the tang of the nearby ocean. Lacy inhaled deeply, savoring the aromatic symphony that enveloped her. It was as if the very essence of the island danced on the breeze, inviting her to immerse herself in its secrets and stories.

As the car continued its journey, Lacy's eyes traced the contours of the landscape, taking in the sights that unfolded like pages of a storybook. Rolling hills stretched out before her, adorned with vibrant wildflowers that painted patches of color against the lush green backdrop. In the distance, she caught glimpses of sparkling lakes, their tranquil surfaces mirroring the azure sky above.

The road wound its way through the heart of the town, revealing quaint houses with white picket fences and blooming gardens. Lacy couldn't help but imagine the lives that inhabited those charming abodes, the stories whispered within their walls. The town exuded a sense of community, a place where neighbors knew one another by name and a friendly wave was exchanged at every corner.

As Lacy's car turned a final bend, she caught sight of the island's crowning glory—the expansive coastline that stretched along its edges. The sparkling waters of the ocean beckoned her, their rhythmic waves crashing against the shore in an eternal dance. The scene was a painter's canvas, an ever-changing masterpiece that captivated her senses.

She noticed Maria pressing her face against the window, her eyes wide. It was the most interest she'd witnessed from her daughter since her announcement of the move. The sight before them was truly breathtaking. The ocean stretched out before her, its vast expanse shimmering under the golden hues of the sun. In the distance, she could make out the silhouette of majestic mountain ranges, their peaks kissed by wisps of clouds. The beauty of the landscape enveloped her, momentarily easing the weight of her unanswered questions.

Chapter Three

Lacy

As she neared the community, Lacy's eyes eagerly scanned the surroundings. Nestled among the lush greenery were charming houses, each with its unique character. Some were adorned with vibrant flowers cascading from window boxes, while others boasted meticulously manicured lawns. Livingston Bay exuded an undeniable sense of tranquility, a place where nature and human habitation coexisted in perfect harmony.

As the car traveled up the graveled path to her new house, Lacy's eyes widened with surprise. Nestled amidst the lush surroundings, the two-story dwelling stood with a quiet elegance. Its pale-blue exterior exuded a timeless charm reminiscent of a cozy coastal cottage. The white trim that adorned the windows and eaves added a touch of crispness, emphasizing the house's well-maintained facade.

However, as Lacy parked the car and stepped out, her keen eye detected subtle signs of wear and tear. The once-vibrant blue paint had faded in places, revealing the weathered wood beneath. The front porch, though welcoming, creaked under her weight, indicating the need for some repair. Lacy made a mental note to secure new floorboards to restore their sturdy grace.

Beneath her feet, the ground felt firm and solid, but the garden plot that stretched before her lay barren and neglected. Weeds had claimed the once flourishing flower beds, and the remnants of wilted plants offered a silent plea for attention. Determined to breathe life back into this neglected patch of earth, Lacy envisioned vibrant blooms and fragrant herbs that would soon grace the front yard.

"So, what do you guys think?" she turned to ask her children.

David briefly tore his eyes away from the screen, his disinterested gaze scanning the house before him. With a nonchalant shrug, he replied, "It's a house," before returning his attention to the digital realm.

Lacy's heart sank momentarily, but she quickly turned her attention to Maria. "What about you, sweetheart? Do you like it?"

Maria's eyes sparkled with a mixture of excitement and shyness. She nodded timidly, her smile revealing more acceptance than her brother. "It's nice, I like it," she whispered, her voice soft but filled with genuine appreciation.

Lacy's spirits lifted at Maria's response. Her daughter's quiet affirmation gave some validation to her decision. She took Maria's hand in hers, their fingers intertwining as they walked toward the front porch. With every step, Lacy's mind buzzed with ideas and plans to breathe new life into their new home. She imagined vibrant flower beds adorning the yard, a symphony of colors and fragrances to welcome them each day.

As they ascended the porch steps, Lacy turned back for a moment, taking in the panoramic view of Livingston Bay. The glistening water stretched out before her, its rhythmic waves crashing gently against the shoreline. Seagulls soared above in graceful arcs, their calls blending harmoniously with the distant hum of nature.

Filled with renewed hope and determination, Lacy crossed the threshold of their new abode, ready to embark on a journey of creating a haven for her family. She stood in the middle of the living room, her eyes scanning the dimly lit space. The bare walls and vacant rooms seemed to echo with emptiness. She flicked the light switch and sighed with resignation when nothing happened. Moving from the living room, she turned on the faucet in the kitchen. Brown-colored water chugged out as it splashed against the white porcelain sink.

"Great. There's no light in this dump," David blew out in exasperation.

Lacy frowned, feeling a twinge of irritation rise within her. "David, please, don't be so negative. No one's lived here for a long time. It just needs some TLC. Once the furniture gets here and we fix the things that need fixing, everything'll be great."

David scowled, a determined glint in his eyes as if he wanted to say something.

"Can I pick my room, Mom?" Maria asked just then.

Lacy smiled, grateful for Maria's interruption. "Of

course, sweetheart. The fun part is, you get to paint it any color you want."

"Okay," Maria replied with a smile before heading up the stairs.

"Be careful," Lacy called after her.

With her hands on her hips, Lacy walked around the space, imagining how to transform it once they'd finished cleaning and their furniture arrived. "All this place needs is some TLC," she spoke with conviction.

"TLC won't turn on the lights, Mom," David retorted, crossing his arms over his chest, his gaze flitting restlessly around the room.

"I know, David," Lacy replied, her voice strained with the effort to remain calm and patient. "I'll head into town first thing tomorrow to get some supplies. We'll sort this out. And your furniture will be here tomorrow as well. For tonight, there's the fold-out couch and..." She trailed off, glancing at the deflated blow-up bed.

"I'll take the bed!" David interjected quickly, his eyes glinting with a rare spark of enthusiasm.

"Fine," Lacy sighed, turning her attention back to the dust-covered surfaces. "You may have to blow it up manually. I don't think there's a pump here."

"That's fine by me." David shrugged.

"It's bound to be cold tonight. Until I go into town tomorrow, we'll have to make do with what we have." Lacy glanced around, searching for a temporary solution. "We can light the fireplace and sleep in the living room tonight. I saw some firewood stacked in a rack out back. I'm not sure if they're good, but we'll have to make do. Tomorrow morning, I'll head into town and get some supplies. We'll need new light fixtures and bulbs. Maybe a fresh coat of paint too. There must be a local electrician who can come out to take a look at the light."

She caught David rolling his eyes, his frustration evident. "Great, more waiting. This is going to be a disaster."

Lacy placed a hand on David's shoulder, her voice filled with determination. "David, I know it's not ideal, but we'll get through this. We're a team. We'll clean what we can today and make the best of what we have."

David sighed, reluctantly relenting. "Fine. This still feels like we've just put ourselves in a far worse situation than what we had back in Santa Monica."

Lacy struggled to find the right words. "Life doesn't always give us what we want, David. Sometimes, we have to work with what we have. It's a lesson in resilience." Turning to Maria, who'd just descended the stairs, she asked, "Sweetheart, can you check the cupboards and drawers to see if there's any candles?"

"Okay," Maria agreed before walking off.

Lacy turned to David then. "Can you please go check to see if the firewood is any good?"

"I can't believe this," he muttered before heading for the door and stepping through it.

Lacy felt her heart sink. David had changed so much in the past two years. Gone was the gangly teenager who would have done anything she asked without complaint. But if she was honest, he had started changing way before that—right around the time his father was diagnosed with leukemia four years ago. She felt helpless, unable to bridge the growing divide between them.

As the door closed, Lacy sank onto the fold-out couch in the living room, her head in her hands. The weight of the situation bore down on her as she fought back the tears. She knew this transition would be hard on them, but she hadn't anticipated David being outright resistant to it.

"Mom," Maria's voice called out to her.

Quickly wiping her tear-streaked face, she turned to her daughter. "Yes, sweetheart?"

"I found these." Maria held up an unopened box of candles. Her eyes canvassed her mother's, concern swirling in their brown depths.

"That's great," Lacy replied, hiding her melancholy behind a smile she hoped would alleviate Maria's worry. She stood to her feet and walked over to her.

"Come on, sweetie," she said, her voice wavering slightly. "Let's start cleaning. We'll make this house a home, one step at a time."

Together, Lacy and Maria started clearing the floor in the living room of the dust and debris that had settled there for the time it had remained unoccupied. They dusted, swept, and scrubbed the surfaces.

David came through the door a half an hour later with his arms stacked with wood.

"Most of the wood was rotted. This is all I got," he informed Lacy before walking over to the fireplace and stacking the wood in the firebox.

"The water's back to its normal color, but I am not advising we drink it. There's a case of bottled water in the car, so we can use it for drinking and oral hygiene. I cleaned the downstairs bathroom so you guys can take a shower. It's really cold, though, so it's okay if you choose not to shower this evening," Lacy informed her children.

"I'm going to take a shower," Maria informed them.

"Okay, sweetheart," Lacy replied. When the little girl disappeared down the hall, she turned to her son and broached another topic. "David, we have to enroll you in the local high school so you can start classes on Monday."

David's face contorted with a mixture of frustration and disdain. "Yippee! I get to go to this backward town's local high school," he spat out, his voice laced with bitterness.

Lacy felt her patience thinning, and her brows furrowed in exasperation. "David," she began, her voice tinged with a hint of frustration. "This isn't easy for any of us. But we're trying, okay? We're trying!"

David crossed his arms defiantly, his eyes flashing with anger. "Trying? Mom, you have no idea what it's like for me. Leaving my friends behind just to be stuck in this backwater town. I don't belong here!"

"David!" Lacy chided.

"Just because you thought this was a good idea doesn't mean I have to like it," he muttered, ignoring the warning in her voice as he stared angrily at the wall opposite him.

Lacy, her heart sinking, released a heavy breath, her shoulders slumped in defeat. "You're right," she admitted, her voice tinged with sadness. "You don't have to like it, and I won't force you to. You have to understand this was a difficult decision for me to make, but I had no other choice. I am trying here, David. A little understanding from you would be great." Her expression was defeated.

David's hard gaze shifted from the wall to his mother, but it slowly dissolved into one of guilt. "I'm...I'm sorry," he apologized. "I'll try to be a bit more understanding," he conceded.

"Thank you," Lacy spoke softly.

"I'm going to head outside and search for some drift-wood by the shore," he informed her, keeping his gaze away from her.

"Okay. That would be great," Lacy encouraged.

David gave a sharp nod before he headed for the door.

Lacy stood in the dimly lit room; her heart heavy with the weight of their circumstances. She was a pillar against the storm, her children's beacon in the midst of their upheaval. But sometimes, in the dark, she felt helpless. And this evening, in the house her father had willed to her, the lifeline amidst the sea of mounting bills following her husband's death, she felt that helplessness more acutely. Still, Lacy knew she had to continue for the sake of David and Maria. She looked around the dusty, half-cleaned room, a determined glint in her eyes. They would make this work. They had to.

Chapter Four

Nikki

"**N**o way we went through that much coffee," Trish murmured, her eyes squinting at the ledger in her hands.

"Have you met our guests?" Kaylyn retorted with a playful smirk. "Half of them would hook an IV of coffee to their veins if they could."

Nikki chuckled, shaking her head as she watched the banter between her sister and the manager of the Nestled Inn. She and the two women were ensconced in the cozy interior; embroiled in the annual inventory check, a ritualistic dance of numbers and bottles and linens that marked the start of the winter season.

Just as she was about to join the conversation, the sharp buzz of her phone cut through the room. She pulled it out, her brows furrowing at the name on the screen. "*Arlington Journal*," she muttered.

"Everything okay, Nikki?" Trish asked, a note of concern in her voice.

"Uh, yeah," Nikki snapped out of her confusion to respond to her sister. "I need to take this," she told them. Her mind warped with curiosity as to why the paper she'd worked at for more than a decade, before she decided to give it up to be by her sister's side a few months ago, was calling her. She shrugged into her coat, not bothering to button it and stepped out onto the chilled back porch.

She puffed out a visible breath of cold air. The end of November had settled upon Camano Island, casting a wintry chill upon the coastal town.

The buzzing of her phone once more brought her back to reality. She pressed the answer button. "Nikki speaking."

"Nikki, hi. It's Veronica," her former boss, the editor-in-chief at the *Journal*, announced, her voice just as assertive as Nikki remembered.

"Veronica, hi. How are you?" Nikki politely replied.

"I've never been better," came the woman's voice, chirpier than Nikki was accustomed to. "I'm Managing Director of the *Arlington Journal* now."

"What!" Nikki exclaimed, surprised. "Veronica, I'm so happy for you. This is a great honor for you, I bet."

"It is," Veronica agreed, her voice tinged with excitement. "Listen, I know you said you needed to be in Camano for your sister, but now that I'm director my first thought was how great you'd be in your new role as editor if, if you want the job." She got straight to the point.

The words hit Nikki like a splash of cold water, both thrilling and terrifying. She could already picture the bustling newsroom, the adrenaline of hunting stories, the satisfaction of a well-crafted headline. But then Paul's face swam into her mind.

"Veronica, I'm grateful for this opportunity but, I... I'm not sure if I can. I need some time to think about this," she informed her former boss.

"Of course, Nikki. I understand. Take your time," Veronica replied, her tone understanding yet hopeful.

As she hung up, Nikki's body slumped against the sturdy porch column, staring out at the tranquil landscape, her mind a tumult of thoughts and emotions. The quietude of the scene was a stark contrast to the storm brewing within her. She had always harbored dreams of becoming an editor-in-chief for so long. That had been a goal all her life. The mere thought of achieving such a prestigious position had fueled her ambitions and stoked the fires of her determination. But now faced with the possibility of realizing her aspiration, she found herself torn.

Her heart tugged at her, reminding her of the newfound relationship she was building with Trish after being distant with each other for so long. Their bond was blossoming into something beautiful. Nikki cherished the moments they spent together, the laughter they shared, and the secrets they confided in one another. It was a connection she had yearned for, and now that they were together again, she feared losing it once more. She and Amy had also developed such a bond that it scared her it would disappear once she was no longer in Camano.

Then there was Paul, her newly minted fiancé. How could their relationship work if she was miles away when they should be using the time together to plan her nuptials?

The sound of footsteps caused Nikki to look over her shoulder to see Trish approaching her with a steaming mug of coffee in her hand. The aroma tickled her nose. Without a word, Trish handed her the cup before leaning against the column beside her. Her gaze fixed on the horizon as Nikki brought the mug to her cold lips, relishing the steam that caressed her lips and cheeks as she took a sip of the beverage within.

"So, who was that on the phone? Who's got you looking like that?" Trish finally broke the silence, her casual tone belying her concerned gaze.

Nikki's eyes flickered with surprise at the abrupt question, and she momentarily paused before bringing the cup of coffee to her lips. "What do you mean?" she asked a moment later.

"Come on, Nikki. You know what I mean. You've got that look," Trish returned. She leaned forward, her eyes never leaving Nikki's face. Her concern manifested in the furrowed lines on her forehead.

Nikki averted her gaze as she asked, "How do I look?"

"Like you've got a really tough decision to make, and you don't know what to do. Like this," Trish replied.

Nikki turned to see her sister cover with subtle lines of worry across her face as her eyes took on a faraway look.

"You're being dramatic, Trish." Nikki sighed.

"Am I? "Trish returned, folding her arms across her chest as she tilted her head to the side and stared pointedly at Nikki.

"Fine. You win." Nikki smiled, impressed at how well her sister knew her after so many years. "There's something I want to do but I'm not sure if now is the right time to do it,' she revealed.

Trish nudged her gently, a silent assurance of her support. "Want to talk about it?" she asked.

Nikki's lips parted as she prepared to tell her sister about the job offer, but she hesitated. Until she was sure about her decision, it was probably best not to mention it. "It's not that important," she brushed off, plastering a smile on her lips.

Trish gave her a dubious look but didn't press the matter. "I'm gonna head back inside before Kaylyn starts to malfunction from looking at so many numbers. She claims she hates math, yet when it comes to determining what we do have in numbers, nothing gets by her."

Nikki chuckled at her sister's playful roll of her eyes as she described her managers love-hate relationship with math.

When Trish disappeared inside, she turned her attention back to the panoramic view that stretched before her. Beyond the border of evergreens, her eyes traced the contours of the distant mountain ranges. Cloaked in misty veils, they stood tall and imposing, a reminder of nature's grandeur and untamed beauty. The peaks seemed to touch the heavens; their jagged silhouettes etched against the morning light. It was a sight that never failed to captivate Nikki, a reminder of both the vastness of the world and the insignificance of her own worries in comparison.

"I'm going to head over to the house. I have some business to attend to and I need my purse," she informed Trish and Kaylyn, who she found in the linen closet checking off items.

"Okay. I'll see you in a few," Trish replied.

"Bye, Nikki," Kaylyn added.

Nikki stepped out of the inn and walked down the two steps leading off the porch as she walked in the direction of the main house. Her breath formed a misty cloud in the crisp autumn air. She pulled her coat tighter around her, feeling the chill seep through the fabric, despite the warm glow of the sun.

As she strolled along the path, her boots rustled against the fallen foliage. She couldn't help but admire the beauty of the season's transition. The deciduous trees, once vibrant with hues of red, orange, and gold, now stood tall and solemn, their naked branches reaching toward the sky. The ground beneath her feet was a patchwork of fallen leaves, painted in earthy shades, crackling softly with each step.

Just as she rounded the corner toward the main house, her eyes landed on the familiar figure on the front porch. Paul was leaning against the wooden railing, his breaths creating tiny clouds in the cool air. The sight of him brought a gentle smile to her face, a silent testament to the love they shared.

"Hey there," she called out, her voice breaking through the stillness.

Paul turned, a bright smile lighting up his face. "Hey yourself," he replied, opening his arms as she approached. He enveloped her in a warm embrace, their lips meeting in a sweet, lingering kiss.

"I was just about to call you," he informed her as soon as they pulled apart.

"I was at the inn doing inventory with Trish and Kaylyn," she informed him. "Were you here long?"

"Long enough. I missed you," he pouted as his eyebrows arched upward, and his eyes became large and round.

Nikki giggled before throwing her arms around his

neck. "Oh, poor baby," she cooed. "I'm here now to make it all better," she continued, planting a kiss against his forehead, the corner of his mouth, and finally on his lips. Paul smiled against her lips. "Feel better?" she asked, staring up at him.

"One-hundred-percent better," Paul replied with a wide grin.

"Good. I was preparing to pull out the big guns." Nikki smiled innocently up at him.

"Wait. I think I spoke too fast," Paul replied, looking at her with a sad puppy expression once more.

"You missed your chance, buddy," she replied, patting his chest before her hands fell to her sides and she took a step back from him.

"You don't play fair," Paul whined.

"Come now, honey. You didn't expect me to make it that easy for you, did you?" Nikki arched a brow.

"No, ma'am," Paul drawled, tipping an imaginary hat at her.

"Wanna come inside? Amy made cookies before she left for school," Nikki offered.

"You know I could never refuse Amy's cookies." Paul chuckled.

The two made their way inside and headed for the kitchen. Nikki placed two plates with cookies and two glasses of milk on the counter before they sat around the island—the aroma of the freshly baked cookies filled the air.

"These cookies are so good. Amy really outdid herself this time," Paul gushed.

Nikki grinned. "She's been experimenting with new recipes lately."

"I'm tasting a hint of something I can't quite put my finger on," he spoke, concentrating on the confection in his hand, as if the secret ingredient would just broadcast itself. "I hope you already asked her to bake the cake for our wedding."

"I considered it," Nikki replied, her smile waning.

Paul studied her with those keen green eyes of his. "Something's bothering you," he noted, a hint of concern creeping into his voice. He reached across the counter for her hand lying there.

Nikki sighed, her gaze dropping to their intertwined hands. "I got a call today," she began, her voice barely above a whisper, "from the *Arlington Journal*."

"The newspaper you used to work for?" Paul asked, his eyebrows shooting up in surprise. "What did they want?"

"My old boss, Veronica, offered me a job," Nikki confessed, "A big job, Paul. The editor-in-chief position."

Paul's eyes widened. "That's... that's huge, Nikki. I'm so proud of you."

"Yes, but..." Nikki's voice trailed off, her heart pounding in her chest. "It's in Arlington, Paul. What about the inn? And Trish and Amy? The life we're trying to build here?"

Paul was silent for a moment, tracing small circles on the back of her hand. "What makes you happiest, Nikki?" he finally asked, his gaze intense.

"I love you, and I love our life here. But this... this is my dream job. I feel torn," Nikki admitted, her eyes welling up.

Paul stood and rounded the island. He pulled Nikki close, resting his forehead against hers. "Nikki," he murmured, his voice barely a whisper, "No matter what you choose, I'll be right here, by your side. Your happiness is my happiness. We'll make this work."

As Nikki looked into his eyes, she felt a comforting warmth spread through her, soothing the turmoil within. She knew she had a tough decision ahead but having Paul by her side made everything seem just a little bit easier.

Chapter Five

Nikki

"Hi, Veronica. It's Nikki."

"Nikki, hi. I didn't expect to hear back from you so soon. Have you considered my offer?"

"Yes, I did. I was thinking about coming back on a trial basis—say two weeks—to see if this is a good fit for me and the company." Nikki paced the living room, the phone to her ear as she waited for Veronica to speak.

"Nikki, I am confident you're a good fit for this job. You were one of my best journalists and you've helped me out quite a bit while I was editor-in-chief," Veronica spoke encouragingly. "I wouldn't have offered you the job if I wasn't confident in your skills. But if you want the two weeks, I'll give that to you. In the end, it's up to you if you want this job."

A smile of appreciation graced Nikki's lips, though

the woman on the other end of line couldn't see it. "Thanks, Veronica. I appreciate your vote of confidence and for accepting my suggestion."

"Of course," Veronica replied. "So, when can I expect you at *Arlington Journal*?"

"Um, just give me a few days to wrap up some things, go over it with my sister and fiancé and then I'll be there," Nikki expressed.

"Great. I'll see you in a few days. I'm happy to have you back, Nikki," Veronica replied with satisfaction.

"Thanks, Veronica," Nikki smiled. "Bye."

"Bye."

Ending the call, Nikki walked over to the window and gazed out at the serene landscape. The sky was overcast, and a crisp breeze rustled through the evergreens. She took a deep breath, trying to steady her racing thoughts. The past day had been a whirlwind of uncertainty, even after her talk with Paul. But in the wee hours of the night, while she lay in bed staring up at the ceiling, she had finally come up with the best solution she thought she could, and she was happy Veronica was on board with it. Now, all she had to do was tell Trish and Amy about her plans.

"Nikki?"

"Hmm?" Nikki responded, turning from the window to look at her sister, who had just walked through the door. 'What's up?"

Trish didn't answer immediately. Instead, her perceptive blue eyes studied Nikki for a moment, which left Nikki feeling uneasy. "What's going on?" she finally asked.

"What do you mean?" Nikki asked, feigning ignorance.

"You've been on edge since yesterday. We might not have been close for quite some time, but I can tell that something's bothering you," Trish said, as her eyes continued to assess her sister.

"Trish," Nikki breathed out. "Nothing's wrong," she tried to reassure her.

Trish's expression indicated she didn't believe her.

"Hey. What's going on in here?" Amy walked in just then, interrupting their tension-filled stare-off. Nikki's eyes averted to her niece. "Are you guys having an intervention without me?" Amy joked. This got the other two women to chuckle, some of the tension dissipating with her presence.

Amy had become such a stabilizing force in both her and Trish's life these few months. Nikki was going to miss that.

"No, we're not. Any intervention we'd be having is to tell you that your cookies and cakes are making us too rotund because they are just that irresistible," Trish jested, her eyes twinkling with affection as she gazed at her daughter. A smile graced Nikki's lips as warmth spread through her chest at how tender the moment was.

"Hey, don't blame the baker," Amy threw her hands up with a grin. "Blame your lack of self-control."

"That's not fair. You know we have no control when it comes to your baking. No one does," Trish reasoned. "Nikki, back me up here." Trish's gaze swung to her, twinkling.

A chuckle slipped through Nikki's lips. "Trish is right, Amy. Your pastries are too good to resist. In fact, why don't we head to the kitchen and have some? I can smell the scent of freshly baked muffins from here."

Amy grinned. "I just took them out of the oven."

"Great. I like eating them warm," Nikki replied, already walking toward the door.

Less than a minute later, Nikki and Trish were seated around the island while Amy placed a muffin and coffee before them.

Nikki lifted the muffin to her lips, the buttery aroma wafting up into her nose. As she took a bite, the warm, crumbly texture melted in her mouth. The first taste was a heavenly combination of moist blueberries and a hint of vanilla, mingling with the delicate sweetness of the muffin batter.

"Mmm," Nikki hummed, her eyes closing in bliss. "These muffins are incredible. I don't know how you do it, Amy. Every time I taste your treats, it's like they keep getting better," she complimented.

"Thanks, Aunt Nikki." Amy smiled.

"See what I mean?" Trish interjected, her eyes playful. "So, how's Gabriel doing?"

"Gabriel's great," Amy replied, but Nikki could hear the hesitancy in her voice. She exchanged a concerned glance with Trish. "I've only spoken to him a few times since he left last week, but I understand he's busy."

Trish touched Amy's arm, rubbing it comfortingly. "I'm sure he misses you a lot," she reasoned.

Amy's lips lifted slightly, but there was a hint of doubt in her blue eyes.

Nikki bit her lip, her gaze going to the coffee mug between her palms. "I... I need to talk to you both about something important."

Trish brought the cup down from her lips and turned her full attention to Nikki. "Okay. Finally. Spill it. You're making me nervous."

Nikki took a deep breath, her heart pounding in her chest. "I'm going to Arlington for about two weeks."

Trish's brow furrowed. "Arlington? What for?"

Nikki hesitated, her mind racing for a believable explanation. "I... I need to tie up some loose ends there. You know, take care of some personal matters."

Amy looked over at Nikki, her eyes wide with curiosity. "Loose ends? What kind of loose ends, Aunt Nikki?"

"Yeah. I thought you had packed up your apartment and moved all your stuff to storage," Trish jumped in.

Nikki avoided Amy's gaze, her fingers nervously tracing circles on her thigh. "I did do that, but...I still have a few things I need to sort out. It's nothing major, really."

"But two weeks? Where will you stay?" Trish asked with skepticism.

"I had a life back in Arlington, Trish. It takes more than just packing up and moving here to have everything sorted out back there," Nikki spoke defensively.

Trish's eyes widened with surprise. "You're right. I'm sorry," Trish apologized.

Nikki sighed, fidgeting with her coffee mug. "I'm sorry. I shouldn't have snapped like that," she in turn apologized.

"It's okay." Trish smiled reassuringly, and Nikki smiled back.

"I'll be staying with Ava," she answered the second part of the question.

"Are you going to be back in time for us to decorate the Christmas tree, Aunt Nikki?" Amy interrupted.

Nikki turned her attention to her niece, her heart aching at the thought of missing something they had planned to do as a family. She smiled, trying to reassure her. "Of course, Amy. I promise."

Amy grinned, her eyes lighting up. "Great. I've been waiting for the opportunity to start a family tradition."

Nikki smiled to hide the turmoil within. She glanced over at Trish to see her sporting an unreadable expression while staring back at her.

Later that day, the smell of freshly baked cookies brought Nikki back to the kitchen.

Nikki leaned against the kitchen counter, watching her niece remove the tray of cookies from the oven.

"Who are the cookies for?" she asked as she watched her niece place them in a jar before tying a bow at the neck.

"I baked them for Sarah. She is going to love these cookies," Amy replied.

"I know she will," Nikki affirmed.

Amy grinned; her cheeks flushed from the heat of the oven. "I hope so. I wanted to do something special for her and the baby."

"She will definitely appreciate it," Nikki assured her. "I'm heading into town. Do you want anything?"

"Yeah. Could you get me a bag of icing sugar and some vanilla? I ran out," Amy requested.

"Of course," Nikki agreed. "Catch you later."

"Bye," Amy replied.

Nikki left before slipping into the driver's seat of her car and pulling away from the house, the car's wheels crunching against the graveled driveway.

Nikki navigated her car through the bustling streets of downtown Camano Island, the crisp air tinged with excitement and anticipation. The town was alive with activity, as people hurriedly went about their business, their breaths visible in the cool late November air. The early shoppers were already immersed in the holiday spirit, eager to get a head start on their Christmas preparations.

As Nikki parked her car, she couldn't help but notice the storefronts had transformed into festive wonderlands. Strings of sparkling lights adorned the eaves, casting a warm and inviting glow onto the sidewalks. The air was filled with the scent of fresh pine emanating from the fir decorations that adorned the shop windows. Some of the more enthusiastic shop owners had gone the extra mile and displayed miniature Christmas trees, their branches adorned with delicate ornaments and shimmering tinsel.

Entering the first shop on her list, Nikki was greeted by the cheerful jingle of bells above the door. As she stepped inside, the warmth of the store enveloped her, a stark contrast to the chilly air outside. The shelves were stocked with an array of colorful holiday-themed items, from sparkling ornaments to cozy blankets and festive candles. Nikki made her way through the aisles, her eyes scanning the neatly arranged merchandise.

As she made her way down the aisle, Nikki noticed a woman standing near a row of winter jackets, her eyes scanning the items with a mix of curiosity and uncertainty. Intrigued, Nikki approached her, offering a friendly smile.

"Hi there," Nikki said, her voice warm and inviting. "I hope I'm not being too forward, but the look on your face tells me you're not sure what type of winter jacket to get, and just maybe you're not used to the type of weather we have here in Camano."

The woman turned toward Nikki. "It's that obvious, huh?" she chuckled.

"I'm a journalist. It comes with the job to observe the little details others might miss and come up with a reasonable judgment," Nikki explained. "I'm Nikki, by the way." She held out her hand in introduction.

"I'm Lacy," the woman said, taking the hand she offered. "I'm new here, and me and my children are definitely not used to this kind of weather."

"Maybe, I can help you with that. I usually buy this brand. It has nice insulation but it's also light and at a reasonable cost," Nikki explained, holding up a coat for the woman to peruse.

Lacy reached out and ran her fingers over the exterior of the coat before rubbing the material between her fingers. "I see what you're saying." She nodded in approval. "I'll definitely be getting three of these."

"Good choice." Nikki smiled encouragingly.

"So, what other supplies are you looking for? Maybe I can point you in the right direction."

Lacy sighed, her shoulders slumping slightly. "I need some basic things like curtains, rugs, and maybe a few kitchen essentials. It's been a bit overwhelming, to be honest. We moved here from Santa Monica, and my kids are having a hard time adjusting."

Nikki nodded sympathetically. "Change can be tough, especially for kids. How old are they?"

Lacy's eyes softened as she spoke. "I have a seventeen-year-old son named David, and my daughter, Maria, is eleven. They miss their friends and everything familiar to them. It's been a rough transition."

Nikki's face lit up with understanding. "I can imagine. But let me tell you, Camano Island is a wonderful place to live. It may take some time, but I'm sure your kids will come to appreciate the beauty and tranquility of this place."

Lacy looked at Nikki, a mix of gratitude and uncertainty in her eyes. "I hope so. It's just hard seeing them so unhappy. I want to make this new house feel like a home for them, you know?"

Nikki placed a comforting hand on Lacy's arm. "I understand completely. How about this? Why don't you let me help you? I know some great places where you can find affordable and stylish home items. And maybe we can grab a cup of coffee and chat some more. It's always nice to have a friendly face in a new town."

Lacy's eyes brightened, a genuine smile tugging at the corners of her lips. "That would be amazing, Nikki. Thank you so much for your kindness. I can't believe I've already met someone so welcoming."

Nikki chuckled softly. "Sometimes, things have a way of working out when you least expect them to. Consider it a serendipitous encounter. Now, let's go find those supplies and make your new house feel like a home. I have a feeling you and your family are going to love it here."

As they walked together, discussing curtains and rugs, Nikki couldn't help but feel a strange connection to Lacy.

Chapter Six

Lacy

"Thanks again, Nikki. I can't tell you how much I appreciate your input back there." Lacy smiled at the woman seated across from her as they sipped the pumpkin spice latte they'd both gotten from a kiosk in the mall.

"It was my pleasure." Nikki smiled back at her blue eyes, crinkling at the sides. Her phone rang just then, and she fished it out of her purse. "I'm sorry, I need to take this," she informed Lacy.

"That's fine," Lacy assured her.

"Hello?...Hey..."

Lacy distracted herself by going through the Camano High School website as she finished off her latte.

"Lacy, I'm sorry, but I have to go now," Nikki said, placing the phone back into her purse and swiping up her car keys.

"That's okay. I understand," Lacy assured her as she stood from the table and collected the shopping bags she had rested at her feet.

"Bye, Lacy. I really enjoyed this. I'm looking forward to us meeting again, maybe over lunch?" Nikki offered.

"I'd definitely like that." Lacy nodded before leaning forward to accept Nikki's hug. The two women separated before heading in different directions.

Lacy stepped out of the mall; her mind still fixated on the encounter she just had with Nikki. The way her blue eyes sparkled with recognition and the warmth in her voice... it all felt strangely familiar. As she made her way toward the hardware store Nikki had shown her, she couldn't shake off the nagging feeling there was a deeper connection between them.

The bell above the door jingled as she entered the hardware store. An elderly man stood at the counter. He gave her a nod and a friendly smile that she returned before turning toward one of the aisles. Lacy scoured the shelves for the supplies she needed. Her eyes wandered aimlessly; her thoughts still consumed by the enigmatic encounter. She absentmindedly picked up a few items, her mind lost in a whirl of curiosity.

"Excuse me," Lacy said, approaching the man at the counter. "I'm new here. I just moved into a house out by Livingston Bay Shore Drive. Do you happen to know any good electricians in the area?"

The man leaned forward, resting his elbows on the counter. "Well, hello then. I'm Tim," the man greeted her.

"I'm Lacy," she introduced herself.

"Well, Lacy, there's a fellow named Phillip Crane. He's been around these parts for years and does excellent work. You won't find a more reliable electrician on Camano Island."

Lacy's interest piqued, and she nodded appreciatively. "That sounds promising. Is his business around here? Maybe I could talk to him about coming out to look at the electricals at my house."

Just as she asked, the bell at the entrance chimed. The store owner's eyes lit up, and he gestured toward the door.

"Speak of the devil; here he is now. Phillip! You're just the man we wanted to see."

Lacy felt a presence behind her, and she turned slightly to see who Tim was talking to. To her surprise, she found herself tilting her head upward to meet the gaze of the towering figure before her. He had to be over six feet tall and possessed a rugged appearance, accentuated by his strong physique, meticulously groomed beard, and an air of assurance as his curious gray eyes looked down at her.

"Lacy, meet Phillip Crane. Phillip, this is Lacy. She just moved to the island and needs some electrical work done."

Phillip extended his hand, a genuine smile playing on his lips. "Nice to meet you, Lacy."

"Likewise," Lacy returned, an easy smile lifting her lips. "I heard from Tim that you're one of the best electricians on the island."

Phillip's firm grip matched her own, and his eyes crinkled at the corners as his smile grew. "What can I say? I'm very passionate about my work," he spoke confidently. "I've been serving this community for over a decade. What kind of electrical work do you need help with?"

Lacy took a moment to compose herself, feeling a strange sense of anticipation in the air. "Well, to be frank,

I'm not really sure. I moved into the house yesterday, but there is no power."

Phillip nodded, his expression empathetic. "All right. No problem at all. I'll swing by your place today and take a look. We'll get everything sorted out. Why don't you write down your address here?" He produced an appointment book and a pen then.

Lacy readily took it and wrote down her address. "Thank you so much for this. I really appreciate it," she spoke gratefully.

Phillip nodded, a friendly smile playing at the corners of his lips. "You're welcome. I'll be by around two. Is that okay with you?"

Lacy checked her wristwatch and realized it was already half past eleven. She had a few more errands to run but was sure she would make it home in time for the visit. "Two is fine," she replied.

"Great. I'll see you then," Phillip nodded.

"Okay," Lacy returned.

With a renewed sense of hope, Lacy thanked the store owner as well, bidding him farewell before exiting the hardware store.

An hour later, Lacy was back at her new house with the supplies she had gotten. Her footsteps echoed throughout the almost empty space as she made her way to the living room. David had messaged her that he and Maria were going to the park, which she had readily accepted, hopeful they would come to appreciate the town a bit more as they explored what it had to offer.

After doing a second round of dusting and mopping the floor, she started hanging the drapes she'd bought. The sound of the knocking at the door caused her to look at her watch. It was ten minutes before two, but she was sure it was Phillip and not the movers, as they had messaged to tell her they would be delivering her furniture and appliances a day late.

Walking toward the front door, she opened it to reveal the man in question, his frame filling the space. "Nice place you got here," he greeted.

"Hi." Lacy smiled before stepping aside to allow him entry. "I inherited it from my now-deceased father," she explained.

"Oh. I'm sorry to hear that. My condolences," he offered.

"It's fine." Lacy waved off his sympathy. "He's been dead for ten years now, but to me it was much longer, as he was never a part of my life." Her eyes widened, and her lips parted in shock that she had just casually shared something so intimate with a man she'd only just met. "Let me show you the light switches and outlets," she spoke up, hoping to dissuade him from trying to get her to talk about what she'd just revealed.

"Okay. Lead the way," Phillip replied with a reassuring smile.

Lacy breathed an internal sigh of relief.

"I'm sorry. It is a bit chilly in here because the only source of heat we've had is from the fireplace. We didn't have much wood to keep it burning though," she looked back and informed him.

"We?" Phillip asked with a raised brow.

"My children. I have a seventeen-year-old son and an eleven-year-old daughter," she answered.

"Okay." He nodded thoughtfully.

For the next couple of minutes, Phillip flipped the switches and tested the outlets on the ground and first floor.

"Did you try the breaker?" he asked after he'd established there was no electricity in the house.

"No. I haven't. I don't even know where it would be located," Lacy revealed.

"I'm guessing it would be in the basement. Where's the door?"

"Um, this way," Lacy directed, making her way down the hall toward the door opposite the kitchen's entrance.

They made their way to the basement and descended the creaky stairs. The air was heavy with the scent of dampness and neglect as they descended deeper into the darkness that enveloped the space. Phillip flicked on a flashlight, the pale glow casting eerie shadows on the walls as dust particles swirled in the beam of light.

Lacy remained at the foot of the stairs; her eyes fixed on Phillip as he swept the room with the flashlight. The dim illumination revealed cobwebs clinging to the corners, their extensive and intricate designs a testament to the long period of neglect.

"Here it is," Phillip announced, the light beams scattering over the shiny box embedded in the wall. He opened it and flicked the buttons inside, but nothing happened.

Lacy watched as he moved away from the breaker and crouched down. He sighed.

"What's wrong?" Lacy asked, noting his frustration.

"Looks like rodents have chewed through a few of these wires," he explained, his voice tinged with disappointment. "Some need replacing altogether." He stood up, brushing off the dirt from his hands, and walked to another corner.

"I wasn't expecting the damage to be this extensive, but based on what I've seen so far, I'm pretty sure the damage continues into some of the walls up here," Phillip expressed as they stood in the hall.

Lacy sighed, feeling a twinge of frustration. "Great, just what I needed. How much do you think it'll cost to fix?"

Phillip scratched his chin. "Well, it's a fairly extensive job. Replacing the wires, fixing the connections, and ensuring everything is up to code... I'd say around $2,000."

Lacy's eyes widened in disbelief. "Two thousand dollars? That seems excessive. I don't know if I can afford that."

Phillip's tone turned firm. "Listen, Lacy, I understand your concerns, but this is a big job. It's not something that can be done half-heartedly. I've been working as an electrician on this island for over a decade, and I guarantee you won't find anyone better. My price is fair for the quality of work I provide."

Lacy crossed her arms, her voice tinged with frustration. "Well, I'm not convinced. I think I'll get a second opinion."

Disappointment flashed in his gray eyes, but Phillip simply nodded. "That's your prerogative, but I'm confident you won't find anyone offering the same level of expertise at a lower price."

Lacy maintained a firm voice. "I'm sorry, Phillip, but I can't justify spending that much on repairs right now."

"That's okay, Lacy. I hope you find what you're looking for."

Lacy gave him an apologetic smile before escorting him to the door. She watched as his Ford pickup drove out of the driveway before disappearing.

Lacy used her phone to find a list of electricians who

were in the area. She dialed their numbers and explained, as best as she could, what Phillip had told her that needed to be done, but each time she was met with disappointment as each presented quote was above the amount Phillip was charging. However, as she listened to their explanations and assessed their credibility, none seemed to match Phillip's level of confidence and knowledge.

"Phillip Crane is one of the best electricians on Camano Island, if not the whole continental U.S.," one electrician sang his praises. "If he's offering to work on your house for anything under $3000, I'd suggest you jump on that because you won't find anyone else giving you a better price," he further advised.

"Thank you. I appreciate your honesty," Lacy spoke gratefully.

She huffed out her frustration. Feeling defeated, Lacy decided to swallow her pride and call Phillip. As the phone rang, her heart hammered in her chest as she prepared for a possible rejection from the man. After the way she'd handled his kindness, she wouldn't be surprised if he hung up his phone the second he heard her voice.

"Hello," a deep voice answered on the other end.

Lacy hesitated before responding, "Hi, Phillip. This is Lacy..."

Chapter Seven

Lacy

"Hi." Lacy stood at the front entrance with a sheepish look as she leaned against the open door.

"Hi," Phillip responded, his expression unreadable.

Taking a deep breath before slowly expelling it through her nostrils, Lacy straightened up. "Look, Phillip. Again, I am really sorry about earlier. It's just that I have a lot on my plate right now, but I shouldn't have shut you down like that," she apologized as her eyes pleaded for understanding.

Phillip looked at her with a hint of understanding in his eyes. "No worries, Lacy," he replied, his voice soothing. "I understand you're frustrated, and you have a right to shop for what's best for you. I can't hold that against you. Let's just put it behind us and focus on getting your electricity fixed, okay?"

"Okay." Lacy smiled gratefully.

Phillip stepped inside, carrying a toolbox and a small package. "I've brought some tools and equipment," he said, gesturing toward the toolbox. "As I told you before, the work will be quite extensive, and there's not much that can be done until those wires are replaced." He must have seen the look of disappointment on Lacey's face because he rushed to say, "But don't worry. I'll make sure you have a room with electricity as soon as possible. In the meantime, I brought some chopped wood for the fireplace, portable lights, and a power bank that should be able to charge up to five devices."

Lacy's eyes widened in surprise at the gesture. "You didn't have to do that, but thank you. I appreciate it." She smiled.

Phillip smiled warmly. "You're welcome. I understand how important it is to have a functional home. And to make your nights more bearable until then, I've also brought a portable heater. It's fully charged to add some more heat to the house, so you won't have to worry about the cold."

"You really thought of everything, didn't you?" Lacy chuckled. "Thank you, Phillip. You have no idea how grateful I am."

Phillip's eyes softened, and his lips turned up in a smile. "It's my pleasure, Lacy. Helping people like you is why I do what I do. Seeing you smile makes it all worth it."

Warmth crept into Lacy's cheeks, and she couldn't help but smile, her gratitude shining through. "Well, you've certainly succeeded in putting a smile on my face. Thank you for being so understanding and generous."

Phillip nodded. "You're welcome. Now, let's get started, shall we?"

Lacy followed him down to the basement and held the light as he worked.

"I'm just going through to make sure that the damage is mainly from rodents biting through them down here and common wear and tear," Phillip explained, his voice resonating in the cavernous space. Lacy nodded in response, although Phillip had his back to her as he crouched in the corner. Soon, they returned to the main floor and headed for the living room. She watched as he examined a frayed wire at one of the outlets, his touch purposeful. "Tomorrow, my men will be here to start the work. Hopefully, we won't have to tear into the walls too much."

Lacy's eyes widened as she absorbed the implications of his words. "So, you mean... there is a possibility that this might take weeks, maybe months, to fix and not just days?" she asked, her voice tinged with worry.

Phillip glanced over his shoulder at her. "Yeah, pretty much," he replied. "It's not uncommon for old houses like this to have outdated wiring that needs attention."

Lacy's mind whirled with a mix of emotions. The realization of the possible work that needed to be done and the overall cost she hadn't budgeted for made her head hurt. Here she was thinking that she would have inherited a ready-to-move-into house with everything up and running, only to find herself depleting the meager funds she had to make the space livable.

"God, I hope that's not the case," Lacy sighed. "I still need to paint both inside and outside."

"Have you already hired a painter?" Phillip asked, straightening up and dusting off his jeans and his hands.

"I was planning to make it a DIY project," Lacy admitted, her voice almost a whisper. The words hung heavy in the air, the absurdity of the notion sinking in as she said it aloud. The sheer scale of the task seemed overwhelming now, and doubts crept in her mind.

Phillip ran his hand over his neatly trimmed beard contemplatively. "Painting the entire house, both inside and outside, is no small feat." His voice filled with a mix of caution and encouragement. "It's going to require a lot of time, effort, and skill. Are you sure you're up for it?"

Lacy's eyes met Phillip's, determination flickering within them. "I know it won't be easy," she replied, her voice brimming with a newfound resolve. "But I can't afford to hire a professional painter right now. Besides, I've always had a knack for arts and crafts. How hard can it be?"

Phillip chuckled softly, a warm smile gracing his lips. "Well, painting a small canvas is one thing, but an entire house is an entirely different ball game," he said.

Lacy looked at the peeling paint and shook her head as a loud sigh escaped her lips. "I simply can't afford a painter right now."

Phillip's brows furrowed, a thoughtful expression crossing his face. After a brief pause, he spoke, his voice filled with sincerity, "Lacy, I can see that you're in a tough spot, but you're only going to wind up paying more in the end if you go it alone. I have experience in painting, and before you say you can't afford me," he rushed out, silencing the protest on her lips. "I'll help you with the painting at no cost, plus I have a painter buddy who owes me a favor, I'm sure I can get him to come in and give me a hand."

Lacy's brows furrowed as she stared at him. "Why are you helping me?" she asked.

"Consider it my way of giving back to my community," he replied with a slight shrug of his shoulders.

"But you barely know me," Lacy argued.

Phillip chuckled, the hearty sound reverberating in his chest. "Do you always look a gift horse in the mouth?"

"Only when it looks too good to be true," she quipped.

"Fair enough," Phillip conceded. His expression turned serious then. "I don't want you to take this the wrong way, but I feel a pull to help you in any way I can. I don't know your life story, but somehow, it just feels like you came looking for an electrician back at the hardware and got me because...I don't know...it doesn't make much sense to me either," he said, brows knitted in confusion. "But yeah...I feel like I was meant to help you."

Lacy didn't know what to say at his revelation, but she eventually managed to say, "Thank you. You don't know how much this means to me. I'm touched." She placed her hands across her chest to emphasize her gratitude.

Phillip tipped his head forward in acknowledgment. "Let me go take a look at those switches in the hallway."

Lacy followed after him, her heart brimming with new hope that everything would work out.

As Phillip fiddled with a switch, Lacy couldn't help but let out a soft chuckle. "I never thought I'd be so anxious about electricity," she said, shaking her head.

Phillip grinned, his eyes crinkling at the corners. "Well, it's the little things that make a house feel like a home, right?"

Just as they shared another laugh, the sound of footsteps echoed through the hallway. Lacy turned to see David and Maria entering the room.

"You're back." She smiled at them. Maria produced a timid smile, but David hardly acknowledged her, his gaze fixed on Phillip, eyes narrowed, and mouth set in a grim line.

"Um, Phillip, these are my children, David and Maria...David, Maria, this is Phillip. He's the electrician who's going to work on restoring light to the house."

David, a scowl still etched on his face, glanced from his mother to Phillip and muttered, "Yeah, whatever."

Lacy's smile faltered, and she quickly interjected, "David, that's not how we treat a guest. Apologize."

David's mouth set in a grim line, as if he was preparing to ignore his mother's reprimand. "Sorry," he finally muttered.

Phillip's friendly smile remained, despite the tension in the room. "It's a pleasure to meet you both. I'll try to work as quickly as possible so I can get out of your hair."

"Okay," Maria's soft voice cut the silence that had descended.

"How was the park?" Lacy asked, trying to ease the tension.

"It was a disaster." David frowned.

"Come on, David," Lacy sighed. "You have to give it a chance."

"Why should I? I didn't even want to move here in the first place. Everything's different, and I hate it."

"The park was nice," Maria interjected, as if trying to quiet the storm brewing.

"That's great, Maria. I'm happy you liked it." Lacy managed to smile at her daughter before looking at David. Her voice grew sharper as she retorted, "David, we've been over this. We moved here for a reason, and it's not going to change. You need to adjust and find the good in this new place."

David's face flushed with anger, and he clenched his fists. "You don't get it, Mom! You don't know what it's like to leave everything behind! To lose everything you've worked so hard for!"

The room fell silent for a moment as David stormed away, his footsteps echoing down the hallway. Lacy sighed heavily, questioning her decision to uproot their lives. She turned to Phillip with a look of embarrassment.

"I'm sorry you had to witness that," she apologized while Maria quietly exited the room.

"You don't have to apologize. He's a teenager, and they're always moody at this age."

Lacy looked at him with skepticism.

"I remember when my daughter just turned fourteen, her mother and I had a tough time. Those are years that whenever I look back at them, I shudder." To emphasize the point, he cringed as his body shook.

"You have a daughter?" Lacy asked.

"Yeah. She's twenty-one now and a whole different person," Phillip replied, his tone full of pride.

"I don't know what to do anymore. He's so angry, and I feel like it's all my fault." Lacy sighed.

"It gets better," Phillip responded, and Lacy gave him a look of disbelief.

Phillip placed a comforting hand on her shoulder, his voice filled with empathy. "Lacy, don't blame yourself too much. At his age, they're often angry about a lot of things. It's a tough transition, but it does get better as they become young adults and are able to see past the stained-glass windows blocking their view.

Lacy shook her head, tears welling in her eyes. "I just

want him to be happy again. I want our family to be happy. But with his father gone, I don't know if that'll ever be possible again." She hung her head in despair.

Phillip squeezed her shoulder gently, offering reassurance. "Give it time, Lacy. With patience and understanding, things will fall into place. You've already proven that you have the strength and perseverance to make the difficult choices in order to protect your family. I mean, look... you chose to move halfway across the country to a house with no electricity."

Lacy laughed at his obvious teasing in his latter statement and the smirk on his lips.

"Just call me crazy," she joked.

After their laughter had died down, Phillip spoke with seriousness and sincerity shining through his eyes, "You're doing the best you can."

Lacy wiped away her tears, searching for hope in Phillip's words. She took a deep breath, determined to face the challenges ahead. "I hope you're right, Phillip. I really do."

Chapter Eight

Nikki

Nikki's heart raced with a mix of excitement and nervousness as she stared at her reflection in the rearview mirror. The early morning sunlight cast a warm glow on her face, highlighting her determined expression. Her blue eyes sparkled with anticipation, and she brushed a lock of her blond hair behind her ear.

"All right. This is it—your shot. Make it count," she whispered to herself, her voice filled with a combination of self-assurance and determination. Taking a deep breath to steady her nerves, she reached for her laptop bag and purse. She swung open the car door and emerged onto the bustling sidewalk.

Nikki took a moment to compose herself. She adjusted the lapels of her tailored charcoal pantsuit, feeling the smooth fabric against her fingertips. The suit hugged her slim frame perfectly and gave her an air of professionalism and confidence. The crisp white blouse underneath added a touch of elegance, and the silver pendant necklace shimmered delicately against her collarbone.

As she turned to face the towering *Arlington Journal* building, its modern glass facade gleamed in the morning sun. The emblem of the renowned paper, proudly displayed above the entrance, served as a reminder of the prestigious role she was about to embark on.

"Nikki, there you are," a familiar voice called out, breaking her reverie. Nikki turned to see Veronica striding toward her with a warm smile. Her salt-and-pepper hair was neatly styled, and her eyes sparkled with admiration. "I was a bit worried you would change your mind at the last minute."

"Hi, Veronica," Nikki greeted, accepting the woman's embrace. "You know I would never do that, right? I am a woman of my word," she affirmed when they separated.

"That's true. I don't know where this undue doubt came from," Veronica wholeheartedly agreed.

"I just hope I'll be able to do a half-decent job as editor-in-chief," Nikki voiced her concern.

Veronica placed a reassuring hand on Nikki's shoulder. "You deserve this opportunity, Nikki. You've worked tirelessly chasing down those stories that kept this paper as a serious contender in the world of journalism. I can't think of anyone else who deserves this as much as you do," she spoke with conviction.

Nikki's lips widened in a smile. "You just boosted my confidence."

"Glad I could help." Veronica smiled back. "Let's go up." She gestured toward the building. The two women entered the building, and after Nikki collected an access badge at the reception desk, she and Veronica entered the elevator and made their way up to the fifth floor.

Nikki stepped into the bustling newsroom of the *Arlington Journal*. Her heart pounded with a mix of excitement and nervous anticipation. The scent of freshly brewed coffee mingled with the smell of ink and paper, creating a familiar and comforting atmosphere she had missed during her time away.

As she walked farther into the room, the clicking sounds of the keyboards slowed to a halt as heads turned in her direction. Most of the faces she glanced over had knowing smiles while a few of them, which she noted seemed to be new hires, wore curious expressions.

Veronica stepped forward then. "Ladies and gentlemen, as you are aware now that I am managing director of the *Arlington Journal*, I must appoint a new editor-in-chief. It also meant I had to hire the best, and I could think of no other who deserved it as much as this woman standing beside me. Most of you already know her, but now I am introducing her to her new role and capacity. Ladies and gentlemen, please welcome the new editor-in-chief of the *Arlington Journal*, Nikki Murphy."

Loud cheers rose up.

"Welcome back, Nikki!" The words rang out, rich and warm, from Ron, one of her previous mentees.

Nikki felt overwhelmed with joy at the warm reception, and her hand flew to her chest as she smiled.

"Thank you all so much," she started. Her eyes scanned the sea of faces until they landed on her best friend. Ava's eyes were lit with intense joy, but there was a shadow of concern in them too, which caused Nikki to quirk a brow.

"Let's get you settled into your new office," Veronica spoke, breaking the silent conversation between the two women.

"Okay," Nikki turned to the woman. Veronica guided her through the maze of cubicles toward the coveted corner office that was once Veronica's.

"I didn't get the chance to change it much," Veronica admitted, her voice tinged with a hint of nostalgia as they crossed the threshold. "But you have complete freedom to rearrange it, buy new furniture, anything you like. This space is yours now."

Nikki's gaze swept across the room, taking in every detail with wide, appreciative eyes. At the heart of the room stood a grand cherrywood desk, its polished surface gleaming from the natural light streaming into the room. A high-back chair, upholstered in rich leather, stood proudly behind it, exuding an air of authority. A cozy gray couch beckoned in one corner of the room, accompanied by a tastefully designed coffee table.

The floor-to-ceiling glass panels presented a panoramic view of downtown Arlington and the distant mountains. The view alone was enough to take her breath away.

"Let's see how these two weeks go first," Nikki finally spoke up with caution.

"Okay," Veronica agreed with a nod. "I'll leave you to it then. Welcome on board, Nikki." Nikki smiled gratefully at the woman and watched her exit her new office.

Settling into her chair, Nikki began to sift through the pile of submissions that had been left on her desk, her mind humming with the possibilities they represented. A knock at the door caused her to raise her eyes to it, just as Ava's head popped through.

"Welcome back, boss." Ava grinned.

Nikki chuckled, standing to her feet as Ava stepped fully into the room. "It's good to be back, but I hate that word, boss. It makes me sound like an overseer." Nikki shuddered.

"Yeah, well, you're the boss now. You have to get used to being called that, especially by the newbies," Ava expressed. The two women walked over to the couch and sat down.

"What was that look back in the main hall?" Nikki asked her best friend.

Ava's lips pursed and her eyes shown with the same concern from earlier. "Nikki, you know I'm so glad you're back," she said. "But what about Trish, Amy, and Paul?"

Nikki met Ava's gaze directly, her own eyes reflecting the depth of her conviction. "I'm trying to make it work, Ava," she said, her voice confident and steady. "I'm not sure how yet, but I'm working on it, and Paul has been so understanding." A soft smile graced her lips as she spoke about her fiancé.

"And what about Trish and Amy?" Ava asked.

"I...I didn't tell them the reason I'm back in Arlington is to take this job." Nikki ducked her head.

"Nikki," Ava spoke with concern. "You do know that this has the potential to blow up around you, right?"

"I know," Nikki confirmed. "I'm trying to find a way to tell them. It just felt like I would be disappointing them by wanting this job." She sighed heavily.

"Nikki." Ava placed a hand on her arm, causing Nikki to look at her. "I've met Trish and Amy and, based on what I've seen, they're not like that. I'm sure they'd support you if this is what you really wanted," she encouraged.

Nikki nodded simply.

"Talk to them before it's too late to come back from this," Ava encouraged, rising to her feet. "I'm ordering Thai food for dinner later," she further informed her.

"Okay," Nikki answered, a weight resting on her chest.

"Promise me you won't let this job consume you. Remember what's truly important."

Nikki nodded.

Throughout the day, Nikki's colleagues stopped by her office to congratulate her and express their excitement about working with her once again. The newsroom buzzed with an energy that was infectious, and Nikki couldn't help but feel a surge of inspiration.

Hours flew by as Nikki read, made notes, and occasionally reached for her phone to check in with Trish and Amy. It was a delicate balancing act, but one she was determined to master.

With each passing moment, Nikki grew more confident in her decision to stay in Arlington.

From her glass-walled corner office in the heart of Arlington, Washington, Nikki peered down at the bustling thoroughfare below. She watched as people, like ants, scurried about on their own missions, oblivious to her scrutiny. The cityscape of Arlington, with its sprawl of steel, glass, and concrete, stood in stark contrast to the serene beauty of Camano Island—she hadn't realized she would have missed that atmosphere like she did. Three days had elapsed since she exchanged the tranquil island life for the pulsating energy of the city, step-

ping into her new role as the Editor-in-Chief of the
Arlington Journal.

She still hadn't told Trish and Amy the real reason
she was back in the city, even though she'd spoken to
them quite a few times already. She knew, like Ava had
said, it was important that she told them why she was
back in Arlington before they found out on their own. She
just couldn't seem to find the right opening where she
could be like, "Hey. Guess what? I'm back in Arlington
because I'm the new editor-in-chief for the *Arlington
Journal.*" There was no scenario she had gone over that
would make it okay for her to lie to her sister and her
niece.

The shrill ring of her cell phone broke through her
contemplation. The caller ID flashed the name "Trish."
Nikki felt a strange knot in her stomach.

"I know why you're back, Nikki," were Trish's
opening words, her voice laced with a surprising hint of
accusation.

Nikki paused, taken aback. "How did you find out?"
she managed to ask, the words tumbling out before she
could stop them.

"Paul told me," Trish said, her voice now a blend of
disappointment and hurt. "He didn't seem to realize it
was supposed to be your secret. I wish you would have
told me, Nikki, rather than lying."

Nikki winced and her shoulders slumped at her
sister's words, regret washing over her. "Trish, I... I'm
sorry," she stammered, her words echoing around the vastness of her empty office. "I didn't mean to lie. I just...I just
didn't want to upset you, especially after all these years of
not being in each other's lives. I didn't want it to seem as if
I was abandoning you."

There was a pause on the other end of the line, and Nikki could almost feel Trish's disappointment lingering in the air.

"I get that, Nikki," Trish replied, her voice filled with a mix of hurt and frustration. "But I wish you would have trusted me enough to tell me the truth. We're sisters, for crying out loud. We're supposed to be there for each other."

"I'm sorry, Trish. I didn't think—"

"And what about Paul?" Trish fired back, not missing a beat. "Is he okay with you being in a different city when the two of you should be planning your wedding?"

Nikki sighed, her gaze shifting from the busy street to the sunset painting the sky in hues of orange and pink. "It's...it's complicated, Trish. But Paul understands," she replied, her voice barely above a whisper.

"Well, that makes one of us," Trish retorted, the hurt in her voice clear as day. "Maybe it's a good thing you did this to save us from greater disappointment down the road."

"Trish, you don't mean that," Nikki spoke, breathless and panicked.

"Maybe it's for the best that you stay in Arlington, Nikki," Trish added, ignoring Nikki's final plea. With that, Trish hung up, leaving Nikki alone with the empty phone and a room full of echoing silence.

She slowly put down the phone, her mind swirling with Trish's words. She turned back to the window, the cityscape of Arlington now bathed in the soft glow of the setting sun. Inside her office, Nikki felt a profound sense of isolation. The excitement of her new post was suddenly overshadowed by the weight of her decisions and the repercussions they held for her relationships.

Chapter Nine

Lacy

F our days had passed since Lacy moved to Camano Island. The house was finally starting to feel like a home. The furniture had arrived two days ago, and Lacy, being a stickler for being organized, had already set up most of the rooms with items from her old home back in Santa Monica, along with adding a few additional touches like the heavy drapes she'd bought that day she'd met Nikki. Some minor repairs and heavy cleaning had also been done to bring the house up to snuff.

As she busied herself with tidying up the living room, she noticed Phillip and one of his employees diligently working in one of the corners. She walked over to them, wiping her hands on a rag.

"Hi, gentlemen. How's it going?"

The men turned their heads at the sound of her voice to look at her.

"Hey," Phillip responded, straightening up. "Everything's going okay. We've identified the main problem now. We've located all the faulty wires leading to the circuit breaker. But don't worry," he reassured her. "Mike and I have got it under control. It's going to take us another three to four days to repair or replace all the damaged wires, and I want to put in a new breaker box as well," he explained.

Though Lacy couldn't help but feel a twinge of disappointment at the timeline, she was grateful the issue would soon be resolved. She was just glad she didn't have to face the dread of having to endure three weeks of construction and tearing through the walls.

Lacy nodded appreciatively. "Great. I really appreciate your help. This move has been quite the adventure."

Phillip chuckled. "That's one way to put it. But I'm glad I could be of assistance."

"I'm heading out for a bit, but you can lock up if I don't make it back before you're ready to go."

"No problem," Phillip replied with a tip of his head.

Lacy gave him a grateful smile before heading toward the door. She grabbed her car keys from the hook Phillip had installed by the front door and called out to her children.

"David, Maria! It's time to go!"

The sound of heavy footsteps sounded on the stairs, and she looked up to see a displeased David stomping down the stairs, Maria followed at a distance, as if afraid her brother's bad mood would spill over on her.

"I don't even want to go to this stupid school," David

grumbled under his breath but loud enough for Lacy to hear him.

Lacy refrained from saying anything but shook her head in annoyance. "Where is your winter coat?" she asked, noticing he was wearing his hoodie, which she was sure would not be enough to protect him from the chilly weather.

"I don't need it." David shrugged.

"David," Lacy said slowly, trying to control her mounting frustration. "The weather here is different. You can't expect to dress like you did back in Santa Monica," she reasoned.

David opened his mouth, ready to argue but, as if thinking better of it, muttered, "Fine," before turning and trudging back up the stairs.

"All right, Lacy, just...keep it together," Lacy whispered to herself as she tried to maintain her composure under David's defiance.

"Mom?"

Lacy slowly opened her eyes and looked at Maria, who stared up at her with concern. "Yes, sweetie?"

"Are we...Are we going to be okay?" Maria hesitantly asked.

Lacy's eyes widened, and her lips parted in shock at the question and the look of vulnerability in her daughter's eyes. Composing her expression, she replied, "Of course, sweetheart. I know it doesn't seem like it now, but as soon as you guys get settled in school, meet new friends, and get to appreciate this town, everything will be okay," she encouraged. "No matter what is happening, you and your brother's well-being are the most important things to me, okay?"

Maria slowly nodded as a small smile graced her lips.

Lacy could still see the uncertainty in the depths of her daughter's brown eyes, and her heart squeezed tight. She wished she could do or say something to make her daughter feel secure. Feeling a presence behind her, she looked over her shoulder to see Phillip standing a few feet away. The two exchanged a look of understanding before David coming down the stairs once more drew her attention. This time, he wore the winter jacket over his hoodie.

"Great. Now we're ready to go," Lacy said triumphantly when his feet hit the first floor. It was David's turn to look annoyed. His attention quickly switched to Phillip in the corridor, and his eyes narrowed before he looked back at his mother.

"Can we just go now?"

Lacy pulled open the door and walked across the porch toward the car. David reluctantly followed his mother out the door. Maria, on the other hand, clutched her backpack nervously, her eyes wide with anxiety.

As they pulled out of the driveway, David quickly fished for his headphones and slapped them over his ears before closing his eyes and resting his head against the seat rest.

A couple of minutes later, Lacy navigated the car through the streets of the town, her eyes scanning the signs for directions. The vibrant shops and cozy cafés, mostly decorated for the season, flashed by as they made their way toward Camano High on Stanwood Street. The sun peeked through the gray clouds, casting a warm glow over the town.

As they approached the high school, Lacy parked the car in the designated visitor's parking area. The school's exterior was a blend of modern architecture and classic charm. Red brick walls stood tall, adorned with windows that allowed glimpses into the hallways. The entrance to the school was marked by a grand set of double doors, flanked by neatly trimmed hedges, and a flagpole proudly displaying the American flag.

"This is nice," Lacy said in appreciation as she and her children exited the car. David, who'd returned his headphones to his bag, merely looked up at the building with disinterest, not bothering to say anything.

Lacy and her children entered the school, greeted by the sound of lockers slamming shut and laughter echoing through the corridors. They made their way toward the main office, where a woman who looked to be in her late sixties sat at the front desk. She wore a friendly smile.

"Good morning," the woman greeted warmly. "How may I help you?"

Lacy returned the smile as she spoke. "Hello, I'm Lacy. I'm here to enroll my son into Camano High."

The secretary nodded and looked through her files. "Ah, yes," she said, pulling out a file. "David Lopez?" she asked.

"Yes," Lacy confirmed.

"Let me guide you to the principal's office," the woman said, rising from the desk and coming toward them. "He'll go over David's transcript and ensure everything is in order."

The secretary escorted them down a maze of hallways until they reached the principal's office. The office itself was spacious with a large wooden desk taking center. Shelves lined the walls, filled with books and awards. The principal, Mr. Johnson, stood from his chair, extending a hand in greeting.

Welcome to Camano High," Mr. Johnson said

As David took a seat, Mr. Johnson reviewed the transcript, occasionally asking questions about specific courses and grades.

David slumped into the chair, his answers to the principal's questions clipped and disinterested. Lacy shot him a warning glare, silently urging him to cooperate. She turned then and listened attentively, occasionally interjecting with additional information about David's previous school.

Once the transcript review was complete, Mr. Johnson stood up, offering a handshake to David. "It's a pleasure to have you join our school, David. I'm confident you'll find Camano High to be a welcoming environment."

"Thank you," David replied simply.

"Thank you so much, Principal Johnson." Lacy smiled gratefully before she and her children headed for the exit.

At Stanwood Elementary, less than three minutes away from the high school, it was smooth sailing in getting Maria registered. Her daughter hadn't spoken much, due to her anxiety, but Lacy could see that she liked the school's environment, especially the arts and crafts room. She was happy at least one of her children was showing interest in making this work.

"Here's forty dollars," Lacy said, handing David the two crisp bills. The coarse wind gnawed at Lacy's bones as they stood in the parking lot across from the mall. She attempted to generate some more heat by pulling her jacket tight around her. "Get yourselves something nice and call an Uber when you're ready to come home. I have a few more errands I need to run," she explained.

David rolled his eyes, a gesture that sent Lacy's heart pinching. "Why do I always have to babysit?" he complained.

"David, please," Lacy begged, her voice a quiet plea amidst the bustling downtown. "Just this once, can you not argue with me? I need you to look after Maria, please."

He let out a sigh, his breath misting in the frigid air. "This isn't once, Mom. It's like the billionth time." Despite his grumbling, he accepted the money, tucking it into the pocket of his worn jeans.

Lacy turned to Maria and gave her a smile, trying to infuse it with reassurance. "Try and have a good time, sweetie."

As she watched her children disappear into the vortex of mall goers, a heavy sigh escaped her lips. She slid into the driver's seat, feeling the cold leather against her skin, and started the engine. She glanced one more time at the mall, then pulled away.

The address from the letter she'd received from Mr. Lynch led her to a quaint house on Utsalady Road. Lacy's heart pounded in her chest with a mix of curiosity and apprehension. She took a deep breath and rang the doorbell, waiting nervously for someone to answer.

After a few moments, the door creaked open, revealing an elderly woman with a warm smile and kind eyes. "You must be Lacy," she said softly, "I have been waiting for you."

Lacy nodded, her voice barely above a whisper. "And you must be Nelly?" The woman nodded and gestured for Lacy to enter.

Lacy stepped inside the small, cozy living room, taking in the antique furniture and faded family photographs adorning the walls. Nelly motioned for her to take a seat, and they settled into a pair of worn armchairs facing each other.

"I apologize for the circumstances under which we're meeting," Nelly began, her voice tinged with sadness. "Your father and I were close friends. He had his vices but he cared about you."

Lacy furrowed her brows, confusion etched on her face. "I don't understand. If my father cared about me, why did he never claim me as his daughter?"

Nelly sighed; her gaze fixed on her trembling hands. "Your father was a complicated man, Lacy. He carried a heavy burden of guilt, and perhaps he thought leaving all this to you was a way to make amends for his actions."

Lacy's eyes widened in surprise. "All this? What exactly did he leave for me?"

Nelly reached into her pocket and pulled out a small key. She handed it to Lacy, a mixture of anticipation and regret in her eyes. "He left you a safety deposit box at the local bank. Everything you need to know is inside."

Lacy took the key, her curiosity intensifying. "Thank you, Nelly. I appreciate your help, even though I'm still trying to make sense of everything."

Nelly nodded, a tear glistening in the corner of her eye. "I understand, dear. Sometimes life is filled with unanswered questions. I hope you find the closure you seek."

With a grateful smile, Lacy rose from her chair and made her way to the door. "Thank you again, Nelly."

As Lacy walked out of the house, the chilly air greeted her once more, adding a sense of urgency to her steps. She drove to the local bank, her mind racing with anticipation and a hint of trepidation. The bank manager led her to a private room where the safety deposit box awaited.

Lacy inserted the key and turned it, the lock clicking open to reveal a wealth of surprises. Her eyes widened as she beheld stacks of cash neatly arranged inside, a considerable sum that left her breathless. But that wasn't all. There, nestled among the bills, was a bank account passbook with her name on it, indicating even more funds were waiting to be claimed.

She sank into a chair, her mind spinning with so many questions and a bombardment of emotions. The weight of a father she never knew leaving all of this to her bore down on her heavily.

Chapter Ten

Lacy

L acy stood in her entryway, clutching the bank book containing her father's inheritance. Her mind was reeling with a mix of emotions—the first was shock and the second disbelief, but there was also a glimmer of hope. She couldn't make heads or tails of why a man who had made sure he played no part in her life would have left all of this for her in death.

The weight of the money in her hands felt surreal as she closed the front door behind her.

"Hey, everything okay?"

Lacy jumped, startled. "I thought you'd left?" Her brows furrowed as she looked at Phillip standing mere inches away from her. She hadn't heard him approach.

"I was just heading out," he informed her. "You okay?" He searched her face.

Lacy's lips formed a hesitant smile, "Yeah... I am."

Phillip stared at her, concern swirling in the depths of his gray eyes. "Are you sure?" he inquired; the words laced with genuine care.

Lacy's lips folded in on each other as she gave a simple nod.

"Okay," Phillip spoke after a short pause. "But if you need a listening ear, I've been told I'm a good listener," he said, his voice inviting.

"I appreciate it." Lacy gave him a genuine smile then. "But for now, I think I'll be okay."

"Okay... see you tomorrow," Phillip replied. With another nod from Lacy, he headed for the door.

"Phillip, wait," Lacy spoke up before he could open the door. He turned to her. "I want to pay you for your services."

Phillip's brows furrowed. "I thought we already sorted out a payment plan. I'm not rushing you to pay," he said.

"I know, and I appreciate that," Lacy spoke up. "It's just that... I have a little money to pay you now, well more than just a little—a whole lot, actually."

Phillip's expression remained perplexed as she rambled. "I don't understand," he responded.

"I know. I'm sorry... I'm not making any sense." She paused and drew in a deep breath, then slowly released it as she collected her thoughts. Looking directly at his face, still confused, she asked, "Can we go to the living room?"

"Okay," Phillip agreed before stepping aside and allowing her to lead the way down the hall.

Lacy placed the bank book on the coffee table between them as they sat in the living room and opened it. The air was thick with a mix of anticipation and vulnerability.

A low whistle escaped Phillip's lips. "That's a lot of cash," he gave out.

"I never expected something like this to happen," Lacy began, her voice filled with a mix of awe and uncertainty. "My father... I never knew him..." Lacy paused; her eyes locked on her hands as her brows furrowed. Her eyes lifted and connected with Phillip's concerned gaze. "He never claimed me, but he's left me all this money." She reached for a stack of cash and waved it for emphasis. A mirthless laugh escaped her lips. "Surreal, right?"

Phillip nodded; his eyes filled with empathy. "Life can be full of surprises, Lacy. Sometimes, things happen that we never could have imagined."

"That's the thing, though. All of this has been sitting in the bank, plus a whole lot more in an account in my name, for ten years. It could have done so much for me and my family..." Lacy shook her head, the pain of what she'd lost squeezing her heart tightly. "I moved to Camano for a fresh start," she continued, her voice tinged with vulnerability. "It's been two years since my husband passed away from leukemia. We were high school sweethearts, and his death shattered my world. I was left with a mountain of debt and the weight of being a housewife with barely any work experience and two grieving children."

Phillip listened attentively; his eyes filled with compassion. "I can't even fathom what you've been through, Lacy. Losing someone you love and facing financial struggles is a heavy burden to bear."

"But it didn't have to be this way," Lacy reasoned, her eyes glistening with unshed tears. "If I hadn't been so angry and resentful, I could have had this money. Maybe I would have been able to afford the best care for my husband, and maybe, just maybe, he'd still be alive. I wouldn't have had to give up our house, and my kids wouldn't resent me for every decision I've made since Carlos's death." An unexpected sob escaped her lips just then as hot tears streamed down her face.

Phillip placed a hand on Lacy's, offering comfort. "You can't blame yourself for how things turned out, Lacy. There is no guarantee in life that the outcome would also be better if the circumstances were different. It might have just exacerbated the situation. Don't let guilt consume you for doing what you thought was right at the time. It can lead you down a very dark path if you do so...believe me." An uncharacteristic shadow of pain and guilt flashed across his face. "It's understandable that you're feeling conflicted. It's a lot to process. Just remember, you have the power to decide what this means for you now."

Lacy used the balls of her hands to wipe away the remnants of tears as she absorbed Phillip's words. "Thanks for letting me pour out like that," she spoke softly.

"Anytime," Phillip said, the corners of his lips curling upward in a smile as his eyes danced with warmth. She hadn't noticed the flecks of steel blue, like glimmering shards of ice, before, but she could make them out clearly up close. Just then, the sound of footsteps filled the house, and Lacy found herself scooting to the corner of the sofa, putting more space between her and Phillip. David entered the room shortly, a scowl forming on his face as his gaze fell on Phillip. Maria walked in behind him; her eyes downcast.

"Hey. How was the mall?" Lacy asked with as light a tone as she could muster.

"Fine," David muttered. "Excuse me." With that, he turned out of the room.

"Sweetie. Why don't you get changed? I'll make dinner shortly." Lacy smiled reassuringly at Maria.

"Okay," Maria replied with a slight lift of her lips.

As soon as her daughter left, Lacy released a heavy sigh. "I'm sorry about David. He's been struggling a lot since his father's passing, and I just don't know how to help him," she confessed.

Phillip nodded understandingly. "Teenagers can be quite resilient but carry their own burdens. My daughter, Blair, went through a rebellious phase when my wife was diagnosed with ALS. And when she passed away, Blair spiraled even further."

Lacy's heart went out to Phillip at the thought of him losing his spouse similar to her. "I can't imagine how difficult that must have been for both of you. Parenting through grief is a challenge in itself."

"Yeah, it was," Phillip replied, then chuckled. "But we made it. Blair's at college studying to become a medical doctor."

"Wow! That's great. Congratulations," Lacy commended.

"Thanks," Phillip beamed.

Their conversation was interrupted by the sound of David's bedroom door slamming shut. Lacy winced, feeling a mix of frustration and helplessness.

Phillip offered a reassuring smile. "It's all right, Lacy. I understand. Sometimes, we all need time and space to process our emotions. Just be there for him, and he'll come around."

Lacy's worries eased slightly as she absorbed Phillip's wisdom. She knew the road ahead wouldn't be easy, but she also realized she wasn't alone in her struggles. With newfound understanding and a glimmer of hope, she looked at Phillip and whispered, "Thank you, Phillip, for being here, for listening. It means more to me than you'll ever know."

* * *

'What about this one?" Lacy touched the fine needles of the evergreen that had to be over eight feet tall and looked hopefully at her children.

"I doubt that'll fit in," David spoke skeptically as he inspected the tree himself. Even though his hands were in the pockets of his hoodie and he wore a blank expression, she knew he was into them shopping for a Christmas tree. She'd seen the thoughtful expressions flitting across his face as he perused the trees on the lot.

"I like it," Maria spoke up.

"You don't know anything. You'd like it even if it didn't have needles," David muttered. A look of hurt flashed in Maria's brown eyes.

"David, that's no way to talk to your sister," Lacy chided. She looked at her daughter to see her staring down at her feet, and her heart dropped to her stomach. "Don't worry, Maria. I'm sure we can find a tree in here that'll be just right for us," she encouraged.

As they continued walking through the lot, Lacy tried to broach another topic with her son. "David," she started, her breath clouding in front of her face as she spoke. "How are things at school?"

The seventeen-year-old shrugged, his hands stuffed into his pockets. "Fine," he muttered, his gaze drifting over the rows of trees.

"You've always been a man of many words, whether good or bad," she teased lightly, her voice barely concealing her concern. "What about the swim team? Any update?"

David's face tightened. "Don't know. Won't know until January."

"That's a bit of a bummer," Lacy replied, her brow furrowing.

His response was a harsh chuckle, his anger simmering just beneath the surface. "Yeah. If we were still in Santa Monica, it wouldn't be a problem. I would've probably had a scholarship by now, Mom."

With that, he stomped off, leaving his mother and sister behind. Lacy watched him go, her heart aching. She shook her head, trying to shake off the tension. She turned to Maria, forcing a smile onto her face.

"And you, sweetie? How's school going for you?"

Maria shrugged; her small frame almost swallowed by her oversized coat. "It's okay, I guess."

"Any friends?" Lacy probed.

"I... I haven't really made any friends yet," Maria replied, then quickly tacked on, "But it's okay."

Before Lacy could respond, one of two women who was about to walk by them slipped and fell.

"Are you okay?" Lacy asked, helping the older of the two to stand the young woman, who couldn't be older than twenty-two, on her feet.

"Yeah. I'm fine." She smiled gratefully. "Thanks for the helping."

"Yeah. Thank you." The older woman smiled, her blue eyes glimmering in the early morning sun.

"You're welcome." Lacy smiled.

"I'm Trish, and this is my daughter, Amy," the woman introduced.

Lacy shook her hand, her smile genuine. "Nice to meet you, Trish, Amy. I'm Lacy and this is my daughter, Maria. The older one is somewhere around. We just moved here about two weeks ago."

Trish's eyes widened. "Really? From where?"

"Santa Monica," Lacy replied.

"Welcome to Camano Island, then," Trish said, her smile warm. "I own an inn here on the island."

"That sounds lovely. Maybe we'll come by one day."

"You should come for our lunch special at our adjoining restaurant," Trish suggested.

"I just might," Lacy smiled.

Their conversation was interrupted by a man who approached them, a soft smile playing on his lips. "There you are," he said to Trish, wrapping an arm around her. "Ready to go, ladies?"

Trish nodded; her lips curled in a soft smile. "Lacy, this is Reed. Reed, this is Lacy," Trish introduced. "Lacy just moved to the island."

"Oh. Welcome to the best town in the Northern Pacific, Lacy." Reed extended his hand with a warm smile.

"Thank you." Lacy smiled, shaking his offered hand.

"Well, Lacy, it was great meeting you, but we have to go," Trish spoke, giving Lacy one last smile before turning to leave with her daughter and Reed.

As they watched the trio leave, Lacy couldn't help but feel a sense of familiarity, much like when she had met Nikki two weeks ago. She shook off the thought and turned back to Maria, determined to find the perfect tree for their new home.

At last, they found the perfect tree for their house and after paying the lot owner, Lacy deliberated how to get it to the car.

"Need a hand with that?" Lacy turned in the direction of the familiar voice. Phillip's eyes crinkled in a warm smile as he approached, his hands buried deep in the pockets of his worn-out jacket.

David tensed beside Lacy. "I can manage, thanks." His voice was as cold as the chilly wind blowing through the lot.

Lacy frowned at David's dismissive tone. "David, don't be rude," she chided gently, her gaze apologetic as it met Phillip's.

With a reluctant sigh, David acquiesced and stepped aside, allowing Phillip to assist him. The two men lifted the tree together, their breath puffing out in tandem as they maneuvered it toward the car.

"I'm sorry, Phillip," Lacy said, her voice quieter now. "It seems I'm always apologizing for David's behavior."

Phillip simply shrugged, his smile never wavering. "It's fine, Lacy, really," he assured her, his tone light.

Meanwhile, David had made his way to the driver's seat, his face bearing a look of displeasure. He honked the horn impatiently, and Lacy sighed. "I'll see you tomorrow," she spoke.

"You bet," Phillip smiled.

Giving Phillip a small smile, she climbed into the car.

As they made their way home, Lacy turned to David, her expression serious. "David, I don't appreciate how you treated Phillip back there. He was just trying to help."

David was silent for a moment before finally speaking, his voice carrying an edge. "Are you trying to replace Dad with him?" he asked pointedly.

Lacy was taken aback, words momentarily escaping her. "How could you think such a thing? No one could ever replace your father," she spoke with conviction.

"Yeah, well that's hard to believe, considering how much he's at the house now, and how you guys keep flirting with each other. I'm not blind, Mom."

The car ride to the house was tense as David sported a scowl, and Maria sat in the back with her head down. Lacy's mind raced with questions. Had she been flirting with Phillip?

Chapter Eleven

Nikki

Two weeks later

That's how long she had been back in Arlington and acting as editor-in-chief at the *Arlington Journal*. The job had been exactly as she had expected: fast-paced and exhilarating, and it challenged her intellectually, having the journalists submit their pieces and choosing what goes to print to be featured in the news each morning. She loved her job, but...something was missing.

The sprawling cityscape unfurled beneath her like an endless tapestry of human activity, a living, breathing masterpiece ensnared in concrete and steel. From her lofty perch within her skyscraper corner office, she felt like an eagle surveying the bustling ant colony, yet she couldn't shake off the feeling of insignificance. She felt isolated.

A gentle knock on the door pulled her out of her thoughts. The door opened, revealing Ava's familiar silhouette against the softly lit corridor. "Hey." Her voice drifted across the space.

"Hey." Nikki smiled as her best friend stepped into the room.

"I have the notes on the harassment case you asked for." Ava held up a wad of papers.

"Thanks," Nikki replied, taking it from Ava's outstretched arms. She quickly scanned through the pages. "This is good, but we need a bit more evidence before we can run this," she said thoughtfully.

"That's what I thought," Ava nodded. "I told Jim to get a few more witnesses to corroborate the story and to try and find out if any of them filed a formal complaint."

Nikki nodded absentmindedly.

"You're miles away again." Ava's voice danced with a hint of concern, cutting through the silence of the room.

Nikki managed a shallow smile. "Just thinking about Trish and Amy. I haven't spoken to them in more than a week," she confessed, her voice barely above a whisper. The names of her loved ones echoed in the room, amplifying her longing.

Ava moved closer, her eyes reflecting understanding. "They'll come around. I'm sure they're all missing you as well."

Nikki nodded, her gaze returning to the window. "I just really miss them and Paul. We talk almost every day."

"Oh, I know. I hear you guys every night." Ava chuckled.

Nikki chuckled too.

"But I miss feeling his arms around me, his face next to mine, and his lips..." A wave of nostalgia washed over her.

"Are you sure this is the place to be?" Ava asked.

Nikki pondered the question. "I don't know," she confessed. "My two-week probation ends tomorrow, and I'm at a stalemate." She sighed heavily.

"Well, you know I'm here for you, whatever decision you make, but most importantly, I want you to be happy, and the life you had back in Camano was the happiest I've ever seen you," Ava expressed. She exited Nikki's office then.

As the door closed, Nikki's phone buzzed, the screen lighting up with Paul's name.

"Hi, babe," Nikki said the moment she answered. A soft smile lifted the corners of her lips.

"Hi," came Paul's equally cheerful response. The sound of his voice brought instant comfort, yet it also tightened the knot in her stomach.

"I was just thinking about you," Nikki expressed as she walked over to the plush couch.

"Oh, yeah? I was just doing the same. What are the odds that great minds think alike?" Paul chuckled, and Nikki joined in as she kicked off her heels before plopping down on the couch and folding her legs under her.

"So, what were you thinking about me?" Paul asked.

"That I miss you," she confessed, her voice shaking slightly, her heart echoing her words.

Paul's deep sigh was audible, even over the phone. "I miss you too, Nikki," he told her. "I miss having you in my arms, threading my fingers through yours, and feeling the warmth of our connection. I miss seeing your blue eyes sparkle when you're happy..."

"Don't stop," Nikki pleaded, eyes closed as she visualized all he'd just said. Paul chuckled again, the deep sound filling her with even more longing.

"I miss your beautiful smile and the way you just light up any room you enter. Most of all, I miss kissing you."

Nikki's lips relaxed into a smile, pushing her cheeks skyward. "I miss kissing you too."

"Is that all you miss about me? My warm, kissable lips?" Paul asked in an offended tone. Nikki could still hear the hint of a smile in his voice.

"Why don't you tell me...what else is there to miss?" she teased.

Paul played along. "How about my handsome face, charm, ability to make you smile, and top-tier cooking skills?" he spoke confidently.

Nikki couldn't wipe the grin off her lips as she responded, "And why should I miss those? There are a lot of good-looking guys with great charisma and superb cooking skills here in Arlington."

Paul didn't respond immediately, and Nikki's heart beat a mile a minute in her chest as she wondered if she had gone too far in her teasing. She gripped the phone tightly against her ear, the silence deafening. Just as she opened her mouth to ask if he was still there, Paul spoke.

"How about none of them are as madly in love with you as I am?" Paul asked seriously.

Nikki smiled, relieved. "I would say that there is the winning point because it so happens that I am deeply, inextricably, madly in love with you too," she confessed.

"Good," Paul replied, his tone satisfied. "Have you thought about whether you want to stay in Arlington a bit longer and give this editor-in-chief role some more time?" He switched to a more serious topic.

Nikki drew in a deep breath before releasing it. "Honestly, I am at a crossroads. I love this job; it's all I've ever wanted, but I also love my life back in Camano with you,

Trish, and Amy," she expressed her dilemma. "What do you think I should do?" she asked in a last-ditch effort to have someone else decide. She heard his release of breath.

"I love you, Nikki, and as much as I would rather you be here in Camano by my side, that would be selfish of me. I don't want my love for you to become a cage. You've worked so hard for this, for your dreams. I can't be the one to hold you back. If you feel that you have to do this, I'll continue supporting you. We'll make it work."

Nikki's lips lifted in another smile, as her heart filled with love for the man on the other end of the call. "I love you," she softly reiterated.

"And I love you," he returned. "Whatever you choose, I'll support it."

As she hung up the phone, Nikki realized it was now up to her to decide what truly mattered most.

* * *

The chilly air of December bit into Nikki's cheeks as she stepped out of her car onto the gravel driveway. The frost-tinged grass crunched under her boots as she made her way toward the house. Her heart pounded against her chest as she anticipated what she would say and what the outcome would be.

Just as she stepped onto the porch, the front door opened and Trish walked out.

"What are you doing here? Trish asked, her brows furrowed in confusion and suspicion.

"Hi to you too, Sis," Nikki ignored the question to say.

"Nikki, let's cut to the chase. I really need to head over to the inn, Kaylyn needs my help," Trish said matter-of-factly.

Nikki chuckled at her sister's directness. It was amazing how the tables had turned. Nikki had always been the direct one, and yet here she was being the one who had secrets, and Trish not being up for it.

Her sister looked at her as if she was crazy.

"I'm sorry," Nikki said between bursts of laughter, holding her hand up as she leaned forward.

"Are you okay?" Trish's voice transitioned to concern as she stepped forward, not able to make sense of Nikki's sudden outburst.

"I'm fine. I promise," Nikki looked up to say, but then she burst into laughter once more. She wasn't sure what was so funny about the situation, but she couldn't help herself.

As if it were a contagious virus, Trish also burst out in laughter. When both women finally quieted, Nikki looked over at her sister. "I've made quite a mess of things, haven't I?" Her eyes filled with regret.

Trish's expression softened. "It wasn't just you," she confessed.

The two women walked over to the porch swing and sat down, then threw the heavy blanket over their bodies to ward off some of the cold.

"I'm sorry I didn't tell you about the job," Nikki spoke, looking over at her sister with regret.

"Why didn't you?" Trish asked with genuine curiosity.

Air pushed through Nikki's lips, becoming a swirling puff of white. "I thought I would be disappointing you for wanting to take the job." There was a short pause before she continued, "I was so happy that we had finally reconnected and everything was going so great, but when the offer came, I was excited but conflicted. So, I decided to do it on a two-week trial basis and if it didn't work out then I could put it behind me, and if it did, then I would have to have a serious conversation with you about it and try to get you to understand I wasn't trying to get away from the progress we've made so far."

"I wish you had told me all of this from the beginning," Trish spoke after another short pause. "Because I would have told you I was proud of you for taking a leap of faith to pursue your dreams. I've always been proud of you, Sis, even when we were apart all those years. I am still proud of you," she revealed, admiration shining in the depths of her blue eyes.

Nikki reached under the blanket and gripped her sister's hand gratefully.

"So, when are you leaving?" Trish asked after their silent reconciliation.

Nikki met her sister's gaze, her eyes filled with a strange mix of resolution and apprehension. "I walked away, Trish," she confessed, her voice barely a whisper.

Just then, Amy sauntered through the front door, the scent of fresh herbs and roasted cinnamon wafting from inside. Her eyes widened at the sight of Nikki. "Aunt Nikki?" she exclaimed. "What are you doing here?"

"I was just telling Trish that I'm back for good," Nikki replied with a bright smile.

"So that Arlington gig is out of your system now?" Amy asked with a knowing grin.

Nikki chuckled. "I guess you can say that."

"Well, I, for one, am glad you're back. Mom has been like a lost sheep these two weeks you were gone."

"Hey!" Trish called out, offended.

Nikki and Amy chuckled.

"But seriously, I'm glad you're back," Amy said with

sincerity.

"I'm glad too." Nikki smiled. The three women shared an embrace then.

Leaving Trish and Amy, Nikki made her way to Lot 28.

"Hi, can you tell me where Paul is?" Nikki asked Magenta, the maître d'.

"He's in the kitchen," the woman informed her.

"The kitchen?" Nikki quirked a brow. "Doing what?"

Magenta hesitated to speak but at the serious look on Nikki's face, she confessed, "He's cooking."

"Thanks, Magenta." Nikki patted the woman's hand before maneuvering through the tables until she was at the kitchen's entrance.

She found Paul at one of the stainless-steel counters, arranging delicate-looking dishes and firing off instructions to his kitchen staff. He looked up then, his eyes lighting up at the sight of her.

"Are my eyes deceiving me, or are you actually here?" he asked joyfully.

"I'm here, Paul." She laughed.

"I'd kiss you, but I need to get this order out," he explained as his focus returned to the dishes on the counter.

"Why are you in here? You know you shouldn't be in the kitchen, in these high-stress situations," she admonished.

Just then, Sarah, Paul's heavily pregnant daughter, waddled into the kitchen, her face mirroring Nikki's concern. "That's what I'd like to know as well," she chimed in, her hand resting protectively over her seven-month-old bump. "Hi, Nikki," she greeted Nikki with a smile.

"Hi, sweetie." Nikki smiled back.

Paul chuckled, a lighthearted dismissal of their worries. "Relax, both of you," he reassured them. "One of my chefs called in sick, and I'm just standing in. Besides, I'm not doing anything I haven't done before."

Nikki and Sarah exchanged a glance before Sarah cautioned him, "You can't keep doing these things, Dad. Not when you're about to be a grandfather and marry the woman of your dreams."

"I know. I'm sorry for scaring you both," he smiled but it didn't quite reach his eyes. "I'll try to stay out of the kitchen." Sarah nodded approvingly. "Now, if you'll all excuse me, I need to properly greet my fiancée."

Taking Nikki's hand, Paul led her to the back of the building, away from the warmth of the kitchen and into the cold December air, but his warm lips were on her before she could get in a word.

"I've missed you so much," he expressed when they finally came up for air.

"I missed you more," Nikki returned with a mischievous grin.

Paul returned her snark. "Why don't you show me?" he challenged.

"That's why I'm here." Nikki grinned. "I've decided to stay here, Paul," she confessed, her breath misting up in the frosty air. "With you, in Camano. I want us to get married soon. I want us to build a future together here." She gazed into his eyes lovingly.

Without warning, Paul swooped her up in his arms and twirled her around. "You keep making me the happiest man in the world," he expressed as Nikki giggled, overcome with joy.

Chapter Twelve

Nikki

"Candy canes and lights? I can't believe you were planning to pass those off as Christmas decorations," Nikki spoke, looking over at her fiancé as they strolled down the street, their breaths visible in the crisp winter air.

Snowflakes swirled gently in the air as they drifted toward the streets of downtown Camano Island, giving it a white overlay. With Christmas just over a week away, the town had transformed into a winter wonderland, with a layer of pristine white blanketing every surface. The storefront windows were works of art, showcasing intricate scenes crafted with care and attention to detail. Twinkling lights wrapped around window frames, while delicate garlands, adorned with ornaments and pine cones, were draped gracefully across their tops. The ice-frosted fir trees stood tall and majestic as they loomed from the distance, their branches weighed down by the weight of the snow, creating a picturesque scene straight out of a postcard. Cars moved cautiously along the slick road, their tires leaving faint traces behind them.

"What? It was either that or no decorations at all," Paul countered as he stared down at Nikki, his green eyes twinkling with mirth.

Nikki's lashes flew high as she stared at him in horror. "What have you been doing all these years...all these Christmases?"

"I'm not very skilled when it comes to decorating. It's hard to believe, I know," he added at Nikki's questioning look. "I didn't want to make a mess of things. I'd rather keep it simple and avoid mishaps. After her mother's death, Sarah used to help with decorating, but she has a lot going on now with the pregnancy and planning her wedding," he finished explaining.

Nikki stopped and looked up at her fiancé, and Paul halted and turned his questioning gaze toward her. Her lips curled into a loving and encouraging smile. "You have me now."

Paul's smile was instantaneous. "Always and forever." He leaned toward her and Nikki did the same until their lips met in a tender kiss.

"I love you," she breathed out as they separated.

"I love you too." Paul smiled.

Nikki's lips split into a satisfied grin. "Great. Now let's get back to making your house a winter wonderland that even makes Santa jealous." She was on a mission to transform Paul's home into a festive affair. To Nikki, the lights and simple wreath on the front door gave the house no character, and she would not stand for it.

Paul chuckled, the sound rumbling in his chest and

bringing warmth to Nikki's cold, pale cheeks. He hooked his arm with hers as they continued down the street.

As they passed by a furniture store, Nikki's attention was drawn to a familiar face. "Paul, wait a minute," she said, tugging at his arm. "I see someone I want to say hi to."

Paul followed her gaze and nodded. "Okay." They walked over to the store, and as they got closer, Nikki could see that Lacy's brows knitted in concentration as she ran her hand over the material of a love seat. She looked different somehow, more confident and self-assured than when they had first met in the mall over three weeks ago.

"Lacy," Nikki called out to get the woman's attention as she and Paul approached her.

Lacy looked up and instant recognition brought a smile to her lips. "Nikki. It's so great to see you again," she greeted in a friendly tone.

"It's so good to see you too," Nikki returned, leaning forward with a curved arm to Lacy, who instinctively leaned forward, accepting the hug. "This is my fiancé, Paul. Paul, this is Lacy," she introduced when they separated.

"Hi, Lacy. It's a pleasure to meet you," Paul spoke with a polite smile as he held out his hand to her.

"It's a pleasure to meet you as well, Paul," Lacy returned, shaking the hand he offered.

"I'm going to do some window-shopping and let you ladies catch up," Paul offered.

"Thanks, sweetie. I won't be long." Nikki smiled and nodded. "So, how's it been? Has Camano grown on you yet?" she asked, turning expectantly to Lacy.

"It's...It's getting there," Lacy spoke cautiously.

"Well, I'm holding on to hope that you'll come to love this place as much as I do.

Lacy laughed then, the sound soft and hesitant. "The mayor should definitely hire you for public relations."

"Right?" Nikki grinned. "So. What're you shopping for? Need any help; pointers?" she asked, looking around the room.

"Actually, I just came into some funds from my deceased father," Lacy spoke with an awkward smile.

Nikki's heart skipped a beat as it triggered a memory of her own father. "Oh, Lacy, I'm so sorry for your loss."

"Don't be," Lacy replied.

Nikki quirked a brow.

"It's a long story, but now I can finally take care of my business and buy some new furniture."

"Losing a parent can be hard. If you ever need to talk, I'm here," Nikki encouraged, placing a hand on her arm.

Lacy's expression softened. "Thank you, Nikki. But to be honest, I didn't even know the man. I'd only ever met my father once, when I was too young to understand who he was. His death didn't mean that much to me because I just didn't know him. I grew up with a loving mother, so it's not the same as losing a parent you were close to."

"Oh no. I'm sorry about your mother too. I can't imagine how devastating that one must have been for you," Nikki sympathized.

"It's been ten years. I've slowly come to grips with it, but I still miss her a lot," Lacy replied, her eyes glazing over with sadness.

Nikki's hand went up to touch her arm and bring her attention back to the present. "If you ever need someone to talk to, I'm here," she offered again with an encouraging smile.

"Thanks. I appreciate the offer," Lacy smiled gratefully.

Nikki nodded. "We could probably trade stories about the type of parents we've had." It was Lacy's turn to raise a questioning brow. "I can't imagine what it must have been like for you, not having a father around. Although, to be fair, my own father wasn't exactly a stellar example of a good one. Neither was my mother. And now they're both gone," she explained.

"Oh, Nikki, I'm sorry for your loss too," Lacy sympathized.

"Thank you. I've had a bit of time to cope with their deaths as well," Nikki smiled gratefully. "We can't choose our parents, can we? But we can choose how we live our lives."

"You're absolutely right." Lacy nodded.

"We're having a Christmas party at my sister's inn on the twenty-second. There'll be a whole three-course menu and live music for the guests. It would be great if you could come, get to know the town a bit more," Nikki invited with a hopeful smile.

"Oh...wow. I'd be honored to come," Lacy smiled, touching her chest. "I'll have to check in with my children first though."

"That's okay," Nikki assured her. "I have your number, so I'll text you the details."

Lacy nodded appreciatively.

"Bye, Lacy."

"Bye, Nikki."

Nikki signaled to Paul she was ready to go and a few minutes later they were walking out of the furniture store.

"Now that our little detour is over, why don't we grab

something to eat?" Paul suggested as they walked hand in hand down the street.

"Nope. Not gonna happen," Nikki said with a shake of her head.

"Why not?" Paul asked with a raised brow.

Nikki paused as she stared up at him with a determined look. "I see what you're trying to do, Paul Thompson, and it's not gonna work."

"What?" he asked, his expression innocent.

"You're trying to distract me from our shopping goals, but it's not gonna work. We're getting these Christmas decorations and you're not getting out of it," Nikki responded, playfully poking him in the chest as she stressed her words.

"You're the boss." Paul smiled widely.

Nikki smiled, satisfied with his response.

Two hours later they walked hand in hand, their shopping bags filled with holiday decorations and gifts. They stopped by a cozy café then and ordered bagels with cream cheese and hot cocoa. Nikki moaned with satisfaction the moment she inhaled the chocolate aroma and the warmth of the beverage touched her lips. "This is so good," she sighed as her eyes fluttered shut.

When she opened her eyes, Paul was staring at her with so much affection in his eyes and a smile on his face.

"What? Is something on my face?" She grinned, running her palm down her cheek.

"No. You're perfect," Paul replied, a soft smile playing on his lips, making Nikki's cheeks flush.

They left the café half an hour later. Nikki admired the way the setting sun painted the sky with hues of pink and gold, casting a magical glow over the snow-covered island.

With their shopping bags in tow, Nikki and Paul paused to enjoy a quiet moment in the town square. Hand in hand, they stood by a beautifully decorated Christmas tree, its twinkling lights casting an enchanting glow on their faces. Nikki turned and gazed into Paul's eyes and asked, "Are you happy, Paul?"

Paul squeezed her hand and smiled. "I couldn't be happier. I'm about to marry the woman of my heart, my daughter is thriving and expecting a baby, and I'm going to be a grandfather soon. I can't imagine life any other way."

Nikki smiled gratefully. But her heart thumped against her chest as a thought that had been on her mind since she came back came to the forefront. With caution in her voice, she broached the subject. "Paul, it's about your restaurant."

Paul looked at her, his brows furrowed. "Is this about the kitchen incident?" When she didn't answer immediately, Paul sighed. "Nikki, I've told you it was a one-off thing. You don't have to worry. I'm taking my health seriously." Tension lingered in his voice.

Nikki hesitated to speak but determination kicked in. "I know, Paul, and I believe you. But I also know that your next great love is cooking and your restaurant. I want you to be happy, but I'm scared for your health, especially with your heart condition and the highly stressful situation of being a chef."

Paul's expression became contemplative before his eyes fixed on her with understanding. "I appreciate your concern, Nikki. Both you and Sarah worry about me so much, and I appreciate it. But I promise I won't go back in the kitchen, not unless there's literally someone on fire, and I'm the only one who can save them," he spoke reassuringly.

Nikki stared at him for a long while. She could tell that he was only putting up a front for her, but she knew. "How about a compromise?"

Paul raised a brow.

"Sarah and I spoke, and we really think you should go back to cooking."

"Nikki," Paul sighed. "I don't want you to feel guilty about me not being able to work like I used to."

"That's not what I'm doing." Nikki shook her head. "I just love you so much and I want you to do what makes you happy. You did the same for me when I wanted to be an editor-in-chief, no questions asked, and I want to do the same for you. I see how happy cooking makes you, and I want you to be happy," she stressed, hugging him under his arms as she stared up at him.

Paul looked down at her with a small smile. "How do you propose we do this?"

"How about you're in the kitchen two days a week?"

"Three days," he countered.

It was her turn to compromise. "Okay." She smiled in agreement.

Paul leaned in and kissed her passionately.

"I love you, Nikki," he whispered against her lips.

"And I love you," she returned.

"After my next review with my cardiologist, if I get the go-ahead, then that's that," Paul said.

Nikki smiled lovingly. "I'll support you in whatever you choose." Paul leaned in and kissed her again.

Chapter Thirteen

Lacy

"David! Maria! Could you guys come down here for a sec?" Lacy stood at the bottom of the stairs, her voice ringing through the quiet house.

David descended the stairs with all the enthusiasm of a reluctant prisoner being led to the gallows. He wore a scowl that seemed more permanent these days, but Lacy saw the pain behind the defiance in his hazel eyes. Maria, who was behind him, kept her distance and took careful steps down the stairs, as if she could sense that her brother was in a bad mood.

"I was doing homework," David muttered as he stood before Lacy.

"I was hoping you two could help me finish decorating for Christmas," Lacy explained with a hopeful look.

"Mom," David sighed frustratedly.

"Just half an hour. Please?" Lacy begged.

After a few seconds of silent tension, David replied, "Fine." Lacy's face broke out into a satisfied smile as he walked past her toward the living room.

Lacy turned to her daughter, who had been quiet the whole exchange. She bit her fingernail as guarded brown eyes stared up at her mother. "What about you, sweetie? Ready to help me transform this house into a storybook Christmas?"

"Okay," Maria spoke softly.

Lacy smiled encouragingly and the two walked toward the living room.

The scent of fresh pine permeated the air as she lifted the box of decorations at her feet, the memories attached to each piece threatening to overwhelm her.

"I don't understand why we need to add more to the tree, it's decorated already," David sighed in frustration when Lacy walked into the room.

"These are the ornaments from our old house," Lacy replied, patting the box she perched on the ottoman. "I thought it would add a little more personality to the tree and make it feel more like a Lopez Christmas," she finished, her voice filled with hope.

David's hazel eyes narrowed as his lips thinned. He opened his mouth to speak but closed it and shook his head before finally muttering, "I'm just helping with the ornaments, Mom. Nothing about this feels like a Lopez Christmas." Picking up the box, he brought it over to the tree and picked through it with a severe lack of enthusiasm."

Her heart ached at her son's words, but she understood his pain all too well. It wasn't the same as having

Carlos here, or being back at the old house, but it would have to do. "Thank you, David," she said, knowing her gratitude was barely acknowledged. Turning to Maria, she asked in a light tone, "Ready to help?"

Maria simply nodded and said, "Okay," before walking over to the tree to join her brother. Releasing the breath she hadn't realized she was holding in, Lacy also joined them.

The family ornaments found their places on the tree one by one, memories of past Christmases flooding back with each addition. The house filled with the soft glow of the lights, bringing a touch of warmth to the chilly evening.

"Mom," Maria's voice barely above a whisper caught Lacy's ear.

"Yes, sweetie?"

"Can we put the angel on the tree now?" she asked, her small hands holding the angel figurine that Carlos used to lift her to place atop the tree.

Lacy's heart skipped a beat as a memory of their last Christmas with Carlos flashed in her mind. He had been too weak to lift a then nine-year-old Maria to rest the ornament atop the tree, but he had improvised, holding the ladder steady as she continued the tradition. It had been a bittersweet moment, but one she wished she still had with her husband.

Swallowing the lump that had formed in her throat, Lacy replied, "Of course sweetie. It's still tradition." She smiled encouragingly.

"I'm going to my room. I've got homework to finish," David muttered, climbing to his feet. Without another word, he walked toward the door, Lacy watching in silent disappointment as he disappeared. "Let's get this angel on the tree." She mustered a smile as she turned to her daughter.

Lacy retrieved the step ladder from the storage room and set it out before the now heavily decorated tree. Maria climbed up the ladder, her small frame reaching toward the top of the tree. Lacy steadied the ladder, her hands trembling slightly as her daughter carefully placed the angel on the highest branch.

The room fell silent, the air heavy with emotion, as Maria gently positioned the angel, its delicate wings spreading wide in a symbol of hope and protection. The golden light from the fairy lights danced upon its porcelain face, casting a serene glow that seemed to embrace the room.

With a soft exhale, Maria descended the ladder, her face beaming with a mixture of accomplishment and sadness. Lacy's eyes brimmed with tears as she reached out to embrace her daughter, holding her tightly against her chest.

"You did it, Maria," Lacy whispered, her voice choked with emotion.

Maria nodded, her voice barely above a whisper. "I miss Dad, Mom. It feels so different without him, especially during Christmas."

Lacy's grip on her daughter tightened, her own grief overwhelming her for a moment. It was the first in a long time that Maria had shared her emotions about her father with her. "I miss him too, sweetheart," she said, her voice filled with unspoken longing. "But he's always with us, in our hearts and in the memories we share."

"I wish he was really here," Maria returned, a sob escaping her lips.

Lacy's arms tightened around her daughter, wishing

she could take away this hurt for her. "I know, sweet-heart...I know." A few minutes later, the two finally sepa-rated. "Let's have some hot cocoa," Lacy suggested. Maria nodded.

The comforting aroma of cocoa filled the kitchen moments later, a small respite from the looming sadness. As they sipped their drinks, Lacy ventured a question. "So, how's school going, sweetheart?"

"I made a friend. Her name's Kimmy," Maria revealed, a small hopeful smile on her lips. "She's...really nice."

Lacy felt a pang of relief. "That's wonderful, Maria." A friend was a start, a small step toward normalcy in the upheaval of their lives. "Maybe you can invite her over for dinner or a sleepover soon."

Maria slowly nodded.

Once Maria had gone to bed, Lacy found herself before the fireplace, the crackling flames casting dancing shadows in the room. She held the last ornament in her hand, a tiny angel similar to the one atop the tree. She thought of Carlos, of the gaping hole he'd left in their lives, and of her two sisters somewhere out there, family she'd never met. Maybe she needed to find them.

"Where do I even start?" she whispered to the empty room, the question hanging in the air as she lost herself in the flickering flames.

In the morning, Lacy found herself heading back to Nelly's. Her hands grasped around the steering wheel as her chest tightened with anticipation. As she pulled up to the quaint little home, she drew in a deep breath and released it. Stepping out of the vehicle, she rubbed her gloveless hands together as the cold winter air bit at her skin. She quickly walked up to the door. After ringing the doorbell, she stepped back and waited.

A few seconds later, the door creaked open to reveal the old woman on the other side, her eyes filled with surprise. "Lacy. I wasn't expecting to see you back here so soon," she spoke.

"I know, Nelly. I'm sorry if I am intruding. It's just that I have a few questions, and I believe you're the best person to answer them," Lacy replied with urgency.

"Oh, you're no bother, dear. I am always happy for the company, actually," Nelly reassured her. "Please come in." The woman stepped aside, allowing her access. Nikki stepped inside and shrugged out of her snow jacket before placing it on the small rack by the door. She then followed Nelly to the living room.

"Would you like some tea, hot cocoa, coffee?" Nelly offered.

"That's fine. I wouldn't want to put you out of your way," Lacy replied.

"Nonsense," Nelly waved off her response. "I offered because I want to make you a hot beverage to give you some time to collect your thoughts and shake off this chill."

"Since you put it that way. Hot cocoa, please." Lacy smiled gratefully. She settled into a comfortably plush armchair as she waited for Nelly to return.

Five minutes later, Nelly was back with a tray and two steaming cups of hot cocoa, which she rested on the coffee table between them. "Here you go, dear." She handed Lacy a cup.

"Thank you," Lacy replied, holding the vessel between her palms and relishing in the added warmth that seeped through.

"So, what do you want to talk to me about?" Nelly

asked after settling in her seat and taking a few sips of her own beverage.

Lacy lowered the cup and looked at the older woman staring back at her with curiosity. "It's about a letter from my father. It mentioned he had two other daughters...that I have two sisters."

"Mm-hmm," Nelly bobbed her head.

"I asked Mr. Lynch, but he refused to disclose their identities. What can you tell me about them?"

"Well, for starters," Nelly said, leaning forward, "both of your sisters live on Camano Island."

Lacy's eyes widened. "They do?"

"Yes. They run an inn back on Blue Mountain Road named 'The Nestled Inn.'"

Lacy's eyes became saucers as her lips parted at the realization of who they were hit her. "Are their names Nikki and Trish?"

"So, you've met them?" Nelly asked with a twinkle in her eyes.

"I did...on separate occasions. But each time I couldn't shake the feeling that I knew them, somehow. They felt so familiar. Th-This is...This is just so unbelievable," Lacy spoke, her hands coming up to cover her mouth as she stared in shock.

"Nikki and Trish are wonderful women," Nelly said.

"I know," Lacy agreed. "They were really nice to me when I met them. Do they know about me?" Desperate eyes sought the truth from Nelly.

"No. They do not," Nelly spoke regrettably. "But I am sure they would be very happy to know you're their sister," she added.

"What am I going to say? 'Hey, Nikki, Trish. Funny story, I just found out that you and I are sisters. Your father was my father too.'" Lacy's voice dripped with sarcasm. "There is no way they'll believe me, let alone welcome me into their lives. Not after knowing I am the result of an affair our father went to lengths to erase."

"You won't know unless you try," Nelly spoke encouragingly. "Give them a little credit."

Lacy left Nelly's, still in a stupor, as her head swirled with questions about her two sisters. As she made her way home, she considered attending the Christmas party after all. The moment she stepped through her front door, she threw herself into housework, trying to keep her mind from wandering.

Later that evening, after her children had eaten and retired to their rooms to finish homework, Lacy found herself standing on the front porch with a blanket tightly wrapped around her to protect her from the icy cold. Her gaze fixed on the white expanse of snow blanketing the ground. She found solace in the peacefulness of the night. But her mind was far from tranquil.

"Hey. You okay?"

Lacy shook her head to clear her thoughts as her eyes found the man standing at the bottom of the porch steps with a look of concern. "Phillip, hi. I didn't know you were stopping by this evening," she spoke, managing a small smile.

"I came to fix those," Phillip pointed to the flickering porch lamps.

"Oh...thanks."

"It's my job."

"Hmm." Lacy nodded.

Phillip set down his toolbox and gently placed a hand on her arm. "Is everything okay?" he repeated his previous question.

Lacy forced a smile, not wanting to burden him with her troubles. "Yeah, I'm fine," she replied, her voice betraying the unease within her.

Phillip's eyes lingered on her for a moment, as if he could see through her facade. "You know you can talk to me if something's bothering you, right?" he said softly, his voice laced with sincerity.

Lacy sighed. She needed someone to talk to about this. She walked over to the patio chair and Phillip followed, sitting beside her. "Actually, something's happened," she confessed, her voice barely above a whisper. "I just found out that I have two sisters... they live on the island."

Phillip's eyebrows furrowed in surprise. "Two sisters? That's... unexpected," he replied, struggling to find the right words. "Have you thought about reaching out to them?"

Lacy nodded slowly, a mix of emotions swirling within her. "I've considered it, but I'm not sure how they would react. And what if they don't want anything to do with me? It's all so overwhelming."

Phillip placed a hand on her knee, a comforting gesture that sent a jolt of warmth through her. Their eyes met, and in that moment, Lacy felt a connection that went beyond words.

However, their brief moment of solace was shattered when David appeared at the doorway. His eyes widened before anger flashed across his face. Phillips hand fell away as she shot up.

"David," she started, but her son only shook his head with disappointment as he disappeared in the house.

Chapter Fourteen

Lacy

"Okay. You can do this." Lacy stood in front of the full-length mirror, adjusting the hem of her deep-red dress that clung snugly to her form before flaring at her knees and cascading to the floor. She ran her fingers through her strawberry-blond hair, trying to tame a few rebellious strands that escaped the high ponytail and framed her oval face. Satisfied with her look, she walked out of her room and down the hall to knock on David's and Maria's doors. "It's time to go, guys," she called out.

David was the first one to exit his room. "Why do we have to dress up for this stupid party anyway?" he muttered, as he struggled with his tie. Frustration etched across his face.

Lacy moved closer to David, reaching out to straighten his collar and fix his tie. "We're dressing up because a very lovely lady was kind enough to invite us to be a part of their celebration, and first impressions are very important," she explained. "Besides, it's always nice to dress up once in a while."

David grumbled but allowed his mother to fix his tie. However, a heavy silence hung between them, a lingering tension from their recent argument. Lacy's gaze flitted up to her son, who was looking anywhere but at her. Taking a deep breath, she summoned the courage to address the elephant in the room.

"David," she began softly, "I know we haven't really talked about what happened a couple of days ago. I want you to know that Phillip and I are just friends—nothing more. I am not trying to replace your father. No one can ever take his place."

David's eyes flickered with a mix of anger, sadness, and confusion. "I know that, Mom," he replied curtly. "You don't have to explain anything to me. It's fine."

Lacy's heart sank. How could she get him to understand that she reached out to touch his arm gently, her voice pleading. "David, I want you to know I respect your thoughts. We're in this together."

He pulled away slightly, avoiding her gaze. "Mom, really, it's fine. Let's just go to the party and forget about it, okay?"

Lacy nodded, swallowing her disappointment. She knew pushing the issue further at this moment would only drive a deeper wedge between them. Instead, she mustered a smile and turned her attention to Maria, who'd just walked through her door.

"Wow! Sweetie, you look beautiful," Lacy complimented her daughter, taking in the light-blue dress she wore.

Maria's lips lifted in a soft smile. "Thanks, Mom."

"Now, before we go, I am asking you both to be on your best behavior when we get there. So please be courteous to the guests."

Maria nodded in understanding, while David simply shrugged with disinterest.

As Lacy led her children out of the house and toward the car, she couldn't help but feel a mixture of anticipation and apprehension. Nikki and Trish were her sisters. How could she broach the subject with them? As she and her children huddled into the car, Lacy quickly turned on the heater then the radio, filling the space with Christmas carols. She slowly pulled out of the driveway.

Lacy maneuvered the car through the winding streets, following the directions Nikki had given her. Soon, the GPS announced that she was coming up on Blue Mountain Road, and her anticipation grew. As she rounded the final curve, the breathtaking view of Camano Island's winter landscape was revealed before her, bathed in the soft glow of the evening light. The winding road led to a vista point overlooking the snow-dusted island and the expansive Puget Sound beyond. In the fading light, the snow-covered fields and forests took on a serene, almost ethereal quality, while the distant lights of the island's scattered homes and the neighboring coastline twinkled like stars against the darkening sky. Lacy couldn't help but be captivated by the tranquil beauty of the wintry scene and she savored the moment.

Soon enough, she arrived at their destination. The inn was a sight to behold, especially with the enchanting Christmas decorations that adorned the path leading up to the entrance. Twinkling fairy lights wound around the sturdy trunks of the evergreen trees, casting a warm, festive glow over the snowy ground. Colorful wreaths adorned with red ribbons and pine cones hung from the lampposts, and a tasteful display of illuminated reindeer and snowflakes added a touch of holiday cheer to the scene.

The impressive wood and stone building stood as the centerpiece of this winter wonderland, its three stories adorned with garlands of fresh pine and red velvet bows. As Lacy approached, she noticed the balconies on the upper floors were adorned with strings of sparkling lights, while a large wreath adorned with red-and-gold ornaments graced the front door. The elegant structure, already inviting in its own right, was now made even more enchanting by the festive decorations that captured the spirit of the holiday season. Above the front door of the adjacent restaurant, Lacy could read the name Lot 28, adding a touch of sophistication to the entire setting, complemented by the warm and welcoming glow of Christmas lights.

"Wow! It's beautiful," Maria exclaimed, her eyes wide with wonder. Lacy chuckled at her daughter's exuberance.

David leaned forward from the back seat, peering through the windshield. "Yeah, I have to admit, it's pretty impressive."

Lacy smiled, relieved to see a spark of interest in David's eyes. "I'm glad you think so. Let's go inside and see what awaits us."

They parked the car and stepped out onto the frost-kissed ground. The air was crisp, carrying the scent of pine and the distant sound of laughter. As they approached the entrance, the lively melody of Christmas carols floated through the air, drawing them closer.

Pushing open the heavy wooden door, Lacy was greeted by a breathtaking sight. The interior of the Nestled Inn, like the outside, was transformed into a winter wonderland. Twinkling lights adorned the walls, casting a warm and inviting glow. Garlands of evergreen hung from the ceiling, interwoven with shimmering ornaments and ribbons. A towering Christmas tree stood proudly in the corner, its branches adorned with delicate baubles and a glistening star atop.

Lacy's eyes swept across the room, taking in the joyous scene. Groups of people mingled, their laughter and cheerful conversations filling the air. The sound of clinking glasses and the aroma of delectable holiday treats wafted from a nearby table.

"Lacy!" came an excited voice. Lacy's eyes zeroed in on Nikki, who was making her way toward her with a bright smile on her face. Her heart skipped a beat. "I'm so glad you made it." Nikki embraced her.

"Hi, Nikki," Lacy greeted back, reveling in the warmth from her sister's hug.

"Doesn't the place look magical?" Nikki asked when they separated.

"It does. Everything is absolutely stunning," Lacy agreed with a nod of her head.

"And these must be your lovely children," Nikki said, her eyes bright and welcoming as they focused on David and Maria.

"Yes. This is David and Maria," Lacy introduced.

"Hi, David, Maria. I'm happy to finally meet you both. Your mother has told me so much about you," Nikki spoke with a welcoming smile.

"Hi. It's nice to meet you," David said politely, holding out his hand to Nikki.

Nikki eagerly shook his hand before her attention turned to Maria. "I love your dress, it makes you look like a beautiful angel," she complimented the little girl with a genuine smile.

Maria's cheeks flushed crimson, "Thank you," she smiled shyly.

"You're welcome, sweetie," Nikki replied. "Come, let me introduce you to some of my other guests," she invited them, her eyes sparkling.

As Lacy and her children followed Nikki deeper into the festivities, they were greeted with smiles and friendly hellos. The atmosphere was contagious, spreading a sense of joy and unity among the guests.

She glanced at David, who seemed more at ease, a hint of a smile playing on his lips as he accepted a glass of eggnog from a woman named Kaylyn, the inn's manager.

Guests strolled about the main hall, their merry voices mingling with the soft strains of Christmas carols playing in the background. Lacy watched as they sipped on warm cider, indulged in glasses of sherry, and shared laughter-filled conversations. The air buzzed with a contagious festive spirit that enveloped the room.

"Lacy, I want you to meet my sister, Trish. She's the owner of the Nestled Inn." Nikki's eyes sparkled with excitement as she gestured toward a woman standing nearby.

Lacy's smile widened as her eyes landed on her other sister. Warmth spread through her chest as she looked at the woman. "Actually, we've met before."

"You have?" Nikki's eyes widened in surprise.

"Hi, Trish. It's lovely to see you again," Lacy smiled.

Trish grinned and extended her hand. "Lacy, right?" Lacy nodded. "I'm glad you were able to come."

"Wait," Nikki interjected, still sporting a confused expression. "How do you two know each other?"

"We met in the Christmas tree lot a couple of weeks ago," Trish explained. "I fell on my behind, and Lacy was there to help me up."

"I'm glad I could offer some assistance," Lacy beamed as the warmth in her chest spread to her cheeks.

Trish's eyes darted to Maria. "I remember you." She smiled. "I love the dress."

"Thank you." Maria smiled.

"This is my son, David," Lacy said, noticing Trish's curious gaze on David. "You didn't get a chance to meet him."

"No, I didn't. Hi, David. It's a pleasure to meet you," Trish held out her hand.

"Hi." David's pursed lips lifted slightly as he shook her hand. Lacy noticed the curious glint in Trish's gaze as she continued to stare at him. David's brows twitched toward each other as he stared at her in confusion.

"I'm sorry. You just remind me of someone," Trish explained her behavior. She turned to Nikki, "Do you remember that picture in the old album, the one of Dad when he was a teenager on the beach?"

Nikki's brows knitted in concentration before her eyes widened as her brows shot up and her mouth hung open. "Wow! Yeah, he definitely has a resemblance to Dad when he was younger," Nikki exclaimed.

Lacy's heart slammed against her chest over and over again.

"I guess it's because Dad just had one of those conventional faces though," Trish reasoned.

"Yeah. You're right." Nikki slowly nodded but her eyes like her sister's remained glued to David. Lacy could see her son's uncomfortable expression as he rubbed his arm.

Nikki spoke up, breaking the awkward tension then. "Let's not waste any more time standing here. There's so much to see and do. This party is all about spreading joy and creating beautiful memories."

A relieved smile crossed Lacy's lips as she nodded. But her heart clenched with anticipation as the secret she held threatened to spill out.

"Thank you, Nikki," Lacy said, her voice filled with gratitude. "We're going to make the most of this night, I promise."

With a nod of understanding, Nikki squeezed Lacy's arm. "I know you will, Lacy."

Lacy made her way to the refreshment table, pouring herself a cup of warm apple cider. She sipped the sweet and spicy concoction, as she looked out at the crowd. Nikki was talking and laughing with her fiancé while Trish was helping Kaylyn serve hors d'oeuvres, a bright smile on her lips.

She glanced at David, who stood in a corner with the glass of eggnog in his hand. Gone was the sliver of a smile she had seen on his lips earlier. His expression was that of a bored teenager who wanted to be anywhere else but here. Maria, on the other hand, sat at a table nibbling what looked like a sugar cookie as an elderly woman smiled at her.

Twenty minutes later, dinner was served, and Lacy was surprised she had been placed at her sisters' table. As she swirled the last of her wine, the mirth and laughter of the party was a stark contrast to the turmoil churning in her mind as her true reason for being at the party warred with her resolve.

"Is everything all right?" Lacy blinked a few times to clear her mind before turning to Nikki, who stared back at her, concern in her blue eyes. "You zoned out for a while."

Lacy hesitated, her heart pounding in her chest. She needed to tell them, to unload the secret that had burdened her. "Nikki...Can we talk in private?" she asked, avoiding her eyes.

"Uh, sure," Nikki agreed.

"Trish too," Lacy added.

Nikki signaled Trish from across the table and the three women excused themselves, with Trish leading them to a private office closer to the foyer.

The air grew thick as Lacy gathered her courage, her hands shaking slightly. "Stuart... Stuart is my father," she blurted out, her voice barely a whisper. "We share a father. He had an affair with my mother...but then he left her. I didn't know about him... about you... until recently."

Nikki and Trish stared at her, their faces a mask of shock and disbelief. "Our father?" Trish stuttered; her voice choked. "No, that can't be. He... he wouldn't."

Lacy looked at them, her heart aching. "I'm sorry to disrupt your evening with this," she said, her voice quivering. "But it's the truth."

"He was many things, but he cared about his image. He wouldn't have had an affair." It was Nikki who spoke this time.

"I'm telling the truth," Lacy pleaded.

There was a long, tense silence before Nikki spoke. "I'm sorry, Lacy, but it's hard to believe our father would do something like that... Maybe you made a mistake."

Lacy's throat became achingly thick as her heart squeezed tight against her chest. "Maybe you're right," Lacy spoke softly. "I'm sorry for all of this. I'm going to go now." With that she turned and hurriedly made her way to the door.

"Lacy..."

Lacy turned to Nikki, noticing the hesitation in her eyes. No other word was exchanged between the sisters before Lacy turned and walked out the door.

The rest of the evening was a blur. Lacy left the party, her children trailing behind her. As she drove home, she noticed David, who had chosen to ride up front, casting worried glances in her direction. His eyes held a question that he finally voiced when they reached home. "Mom, are you okay?" he asked, his voice thick with concern.

"Yes, David, I'm fine," she answered, forcing a smile. But she could see in his eyes that he didn't believe her. All she wanted was to be alone.

She retreated to her room, closing the door gently behind her. The moment she was alone, the dam broke. Silent tears streamed down her face as she sank to the floor, her body wracked with sobs. She felt alone, utterly isolated in her grief.

Chapter Fifteen

Nikki

Nikki's eyelids fluttered open, only to be met with a pounding headache that seemed to reverberate through her skull. "Ugh", she groaned as she gingerly sat up, her mind foggy with the remnants of the Christmas party from the night before. The laughter, the clinking of glasses, and the merriment seemed distant now, overshadowed by Lacy's unexpected revelation.

"I'm your sister." Her heart clenched with trepidation of what that statement could mean for already painful memory of hers and Trish's childhood and their father. The claim they had another sister had shaken Nikki and Trish to the core, leaving them in a state of disbelief and confusion. Nikki's memories of the conversation with Lacy played on a loop in her mind, each word etching itself deeper into her consciousness.

Denial had been Nikki's initial reaction. She had almost accused Lacy of lying, unable to fathom the idea that their family tree had a hidden branch. The weight of her doubt had been palpable, hanging heavily in the air as Lacy's face registered a mix of hope and vulnerability. Nikki's heart ached as she recalled the flicker of pain in Lacy's eyes, the desperate need to be believed.

But as Nikki rose from the bed and made her way to the bathroom, the nagging feeling of uncertainty gnawed at her as she remembered her conversation with Lacy prior to last night. What if she was telling the truth?

Slowly, she got out of bed and made her way to the bathroom. Reaching for the aspirin bottle, she popped a couple of pills into her mouth, chasing them down with a sip of water. The bitterness of the medication seemed to mirror the bitterness of her doubts, leaving a lingering taste of uncertainty.

With a sigh, she ventured toward the kitchen, her head still throbbing with each step. The scent of cinnamon and other warm spices wafted through the air, curling around her senses like a familiar embrace. Pushing open the kitchen door, the scent of cinnamon and spices enveloped her, mingling with the familiar notes of Christmas carols playing softly from the radio.

"Good morning." Amy who stood at the counter rolling cookie dough, a cloud of flour dusting her apron, greeted with a warm smile on her face.

"Good morning, Amy," Nikki croaked as she took a seat by the island.

"You sound awful," Amy concluded. "You don't look too good either."

Nikki managed a weak smile, her eyes reflecting the

remnants of her headache. "Head's pounding, but I'll survive."

Amy nodded in understanding. "Some coffee might do the trick," she suggested, already dusting the flour from her hands and reaching for a mug from the cupboard and pouring the hot, dark liquid from the receptacle.

"I think you might be right," Nikki agreed. She readily accepted the steaming beverage. The aroma of freshly brewed coffee, mingled with the holiday spices, offered solace in its warmth. Heat seep into her hands as she took a cautious sip. The rich flavor danced across her tongue, soothing her senses, and clearing away some of the mental fog that had clouded her thoughts.

As Nikki savored the coffee, her gaze wandered to the counter, where a tray of sugar cookies sat cooling. They were perfectly golden and adorned with delicate sprinkles.

Amy followed her gaze and a mischievous smile played on her lips. "You should try one. They're my specialty," she said bringing the tray closer to her aunt.

"Everything is your specialty." Nikki smiled.

Amy's lips curved into a genuine smile as Nikki reached for a cookie. The soft, melt-in-your-mouth texture contrasted with the gentle crunch of the sprinkles, creating a symphony of flavors. She took a bite and closed her eyes, savoring the moment.

"Mmm...these are amazing," Nikki complimented, her voice laced with appreciation. "You've really outdone yourself."

Amy's smile widened, her eyes twinkling with a mixture of pride and curiosity. "Thanks, Aunt Nikki."

Nikki smiled encouragingly. "Where's Trish? I

thought she'd be here." Her eyes darted around the room, as if expecting her sister to magically appear.

Amy turned, a knowing look in her eyes as she wiped her hands on a dishcloth. "Mom got an emergency call from Kaylyn. She had to rush over to the inn. Is everything all right?"

Nikki's brow furrowed with concern, but she shook her head. "I'm not sure. We had a... surprising revelation last night. It's been a lot to process." She paused, her gaze shifting away as she recalled the conversation with Lacy.

"Come on, Aunt Nikki. Spill it. What happened at the party that has you and Mom looking so out of it? You can't just leave me hanging," Amy urged.

Nikki hesitated, her mind grappling with the weight of last night's revelation. But she didn't want to lie or keep secrets from her niece. Plenty of that had gone around as it is.

"A woman we met...I think you've met her too. Well... she showed up at the party last night," Nikki confessed softly, her gaze fixed on the swirling patterns in her coffee cup. "She claimed to be our sister. Trish and I... we didn't know what to think. It caught us completely off guard."

Amy's eyes widened. "What?" Her hand instinctively reached up to grasp her neck. "That's...Do you believe her?"

Nikki sighed. "She claimed our dad had an affair with her mother. Trish and I... we were in shock. It's hard to believe, but something in me is telling me that it might be true."

"Wow," Amy muttered, her expression still stunned. "This is a lot to take in." Shaking her head, she continued, "Being a part of this family keeps getting interesting."

Nikki gave her a rueful smile. "Hopefully, there aren't

any more secrets to unearth, or better yet, unknown family members waiting to pop out of the woodwork.

"Hopefully," Amy agreed.

"So, who are the cookies for?" Nikki asked, changing the subject.

"They're for Lot 28. Paul said the guests really loved them so he's coming to pick them up in a few.

"Look at you, already making a stir in the world of pastry. I'm proud of you," Nikki beamed with pride.

Amy's smile was equally wide. "Well, you know, I try." The two shared a chuckle before Nikki retired to the living room to catch up on some reading and to make a call to her best friend.

"Brrr. This room is freezing." Nikki shivered as she stepped into the room. Walking over to the fireplace, she stacked a few pieces of wood into the firebox before lighting it.

As the crackling flames grew, their radiant heat began to dispel the chill that had settled. Nikki sank into the welcoming embrace of the plush couch, her skin tingling as the room transformed into a haven of coziness and comfort. She closed her eyes, letting out a contented sigh as the toasty warmth wrapped around her like a soft, comforting blanket. The Christmas tree, less than a foot away from the fireplace, was adorned with glimmering lights and delicate ornaments. Nikki wasn't sure, but the scent of the pine seemed stronger as it mingled with the aroma of the crackling fire. The soothing sound and scents created a tranquil ambiance that lulled her into a state of relaxation and, before she knew it, she was out.

"Nikki..."

Nikki's eyes slowly opened, adjusting to the light in the room before they focused on a smiling face above hers.

"Hi," Paul said, his voice infused with tenderness as he brushed a gentle hand across her cheek.

"Hi," Nikki replied, her voice still heavy with drowsiness as she shifted to sit up. "How long have you been standing there?" she asked, arching her back in a luxurious stretch.

"Long enough," Paul said with a hint of playfulness, "You looked so peaceful, I didn't want to disturb you."

Nikki's eyes sparkled with amusement, as she reached out to playfully swat his arm. "You're such a sneak," she teased, a soft chuckle escaping her.

Paul grinned, his gaze lingering on her. "I couldn't resist," he admitted, his voice filled with warmth, "You look so beautiful when you're sleeping."

Blushing, Nikki's gaze dropped momentarily before she met his eyes again, her heart swelling with affection. "Is this going to be a regular occurrence after we're married?"

"Of course. Your face is the first thing I want to see when I wake up and the last when I go to sleep," Paul confessed as he leaned down to capture her lips in a tender kiss.

"That's all I wanted to hear," Nikki smiled as they separated. "How's Sarah doing?" she asked with concern. "I heard she's on leave from the hospital."

Paul sighed, his eyes reflecting a mix of worry and weariness. "Yeah, her pregnancy has become a risk. Her OB/GYN thought it would be best for her to take some time off."

"It's for the best," Nikki said encouragingly.

Paul sighed again. "Tell that to her. She's miserable because she can't be at the hospital."

"That's because she's a workaholic like her dad,"

Nikki reasoned. "But that's because you're both so passionate about what you do."

Paul bobbed his head. "I guess you're right."

"Everything'll be fine." Nikki, sensing his unease, smiled reassuringly.

Paul nodded appreciatively, his hand reaching out to intertwine with Nikki's. "So, about last night..."

Nikki's stomach pitted into tight coils.

"Have you heard back from Lacy?" Paul asked.

"No...I haven't," she softly answered. "I just can't see my dad doing such a thing as having an affair. He was no saint, but his image meant everything to him. I just can't see him doing anything to jeopardize that."

"But?" Paul prompted.

"Something inside is telling me to believe Lacy," she revealed.

"I think you should trust your instinct," Paul returned.

A noise in the hallway caught their attention. Trish walked into the room then. "Hi, guys," she greeted.

"Hi, Trish," Paul greeted back.

"Is everything okay at the inn?" Nikki asked.

"Yeah. There was a clogged toilet and some missing linen. But that's all sorted out now," Trish responded.

"Okay. That's good." Nikki nodded appreciatively.

"I'll leave you two to talk," Paul spoke, rising from the couch. After sharing another kiss with Nikki, he left.

"I've been thinking about last night a lot," Trish started walking over to the couch and sitting down.

"Me too," Nikki revealed.

Trish sighed, her voice laced with a mixture of unease and curiosity. "It's like... It's like a door has been opened, and now that it is, there's no way to shut it until we'd have all the facts."

Nikki nodded, her own thoughts echoing her sister's sentiments. "I know exactly what you mean. It's hard to ignore the possibility that we've been missing out on something all these years. But...it's also scary to think Dad was that treacherous."

"Believe me, when it comes to Dad, I have no illusions of who he was," Trish countered.

"I know who we can ask about Dad's alleged affair," Nikki spoke.

Trish's brows lifted. "Who?"

"Nelly."

Chapter Sixteen

Nikki

Nikki's heart raced with anticipation. Her fingers tapped wildly against her leg as she waited for Nelly to arrive. The old woman had agreed to tell them everything she knew but had insisted they talk in person.

"How are you feeling?" Paul, who sat beside her on the couch, leaned over and asked. His voice was filled with a gentle concern as his warm green eyes met hers.

Nikki took a deep breath, her heart pounding in her chest. "Honestly...I'm nervous. I mean, after all these years and now finding out we might actually have a sister...it's like everything we thought we knew has been turned upside down."

Paul reached out and gently cupped her trembling hand in his. "I know it's a lot, but remember I'm here with you, and I'll be here after Nelly says her piece," he assured her.

"Thanks. I needed to hear that, and I need you here." Nikki smiled appreciatively.

Just as their hands interlocked, the doorbell chimed. Nikki's heart skipped a beat and she exchanged looks of panic with Trish, who sat across from them.

"I'll get it," she said, rising to her feet. As she walked toward the door, she was sure she could hear her wildly beating heart. Her feet felt like lead and the closer she got to the door, the more terrified she felt. Finally, she made it to the door and slowly pulled it open.

Nelly stood before her. The old woman's face was lightly etched with wrinkles, but her eyes twinkled with wisdom and kindness. She was bundled up in a warm winter coat, a light dusting of snow on it.

"Hi, Nelly," Nikki greeted. Her voice quivered slightly. She stepped aside to grant her access. "Thank you for agreeing to meet with Trish and me."

"It's only fair I meet with you both. I know you must have a lot of questions. I'll answer them as best I can," Nelly replied.

"I really do appreciate you coming here today though," Nikki returned.

Nelly smiled warmly, her voice carrying a hint of a nostalgic tremor. "I've known your father for a long time, Nikki. It's only fair that I share what I know."

As Nelly shuffled into the living room, Trish and Paul rose from their seats, their eyes fixed on the old woman.

"Hi, Nelly. I'm glad you could make it," Trish greeted.

Nelly smiled. "The pleasure is all mine, dear."

Once settled, Nelly cleared her throat. "Before I begin, I want you to know that I did not keep this information from you to deceive you, but at the time it was not mine to share."

"We understand, Nelly. Please, tell us, do we really have a sister we knew nothing about?" Trish asked, her impatience getting the best of her."

Nelly's eyes softened, and she nodded. "Yes, it's true."

Nikki felt like someone had dropped an anvil weighing more than a ton directly on her chest.

"Your father, God rest his soul, did in fact have a secret daughter. He kept this hidden from everyone, including your mother."

"H-h-how could he do that to us?" Nikki asked, her voice filled with confusion and anger.

Nelly looked between the siblings before continuing, "Your father was a complex man."

"Controlling," Trish responded, her voice dripping with disdain. "How about he was controlling, manipulative, and cold as ice? Do you know the things he made Nikki and I do just to maintain his image?" she seethed. "I had to give my own daughter up for adoption!"

Nikki walked over and sat beside Trish, whose body radiated with anger. Gently, she moved her palm back and forth over her back.

"I'm sorry," Trish apologized. "I didn't re—I...it's just the thought of my father sometimes rubs me the wrong way."

"That's fine," Nelly spoke reassuringly.

"We've always resented him for how he treated us," Nikki expressed. "We never understood why..."

Nelly nodded her understanding. "A long, long time ago, I found your father, Stuart, on the beach. He was drunk as a skunk and had a look of desperation in his eyes."

Nikki's brows furrowed at the image of her father drowning his sorrows by the shore. She exchanged a glance with Trish, question mirrored in each other's eyes.

"He confessed to me that he had just found out he had cancer," Nelly continued, her voice filled with a mixture of sadness and recollection. "But that wasn't the only thing he revealed. He said he had done something stupid—a mistake he deeply regretted."

The room fell into a heavy silence, the weight of Nelly's words hanging in the air. Nikki's mind raced, searching for answers in the fragments of their father's past.

"He told me he had an affair," Nelly continued, her voice barely above a whisper. "But he ended it. He thought it was over until he discovered he had a daughter."

Nikki's breath caught in her throat at the confirmation. A sister. Lacy's words echoed in her mind, "I'm your sister." They actually had a sister, a flesh-and-blood half sibling, connected to them.

"He only met her once," Nelly revealed, her voice laced with sorrow. "He sent money to support her, but the mother mailed it back to him."

Tears welled up in Nikki's eyes as the weight of Nelly's words settled on her shoulders. The truth they had been denied for so long finally emerged like an untangled knot, revealing a hidden path. She clung to Paul's hand, seeking solace and support.

Nelly's gaze shifted between the siblings; her voice filled with compassion. "Your father enlisted my help, you see. He wanted to make amends, to ensure that Lacy had something to remember him by. So, we set up an account for her and he left her a property he had in Livingston Bay."

Nikki's mind reeled, as she continued processing the enormity of the revelation. Lacy was real and she was living on Camano Island.

The soft snow was beginning to crunch underfoot as Nikki, Trish, and Amy strolled through the bustling town of Camano Island. It was two days before Christmas. There was a sense of anticipation and joy in the air, but the festive cheer, the colorful decorations, and the carols floating through the air felt at odds with the tumultuous feelings that stirred in Nikki's heart.

As they navigated the throng of last-minute shoppers, Nikki found herself wrestling with the revelations that had recently rocked her world—their father had been dying of cancer before the scuba diving accident that had taken his and their mother's lives. And more significantly, he had had an affair that had resulted in a daughter, Lacy, their half sister.

"How could he keep so much from us, Trish?" Nikki voiced out, her words barely a whisper amid the festive hustle and bustle. "How could Dad have had an affair, a child, and kept it from us?"

Trish's expression mirrored Nikki's turmoil, her forehead creased with deep lines of concern. She reached for Nikki's hand, providing a gentle reassurance. "I know, Nikki. It's a lot to process. We thought we knew who our parents were, but now it feels like we're discovering an entirely different and more disturbing side to them. It's confusing and over-whelming.

Stuart had always been a controlling figure, often making them do things they didn't agree with to maintain his image. But these new revelations painted a picture of a man they barely recognized.

Nikki nodded, her eyes clouded with a mixture of anger, disbelief, and sadness. "And poor Lacy... to grow up without a father while we had both parents in our lives. It feels so unfair, and it breaks my heart."

Trish's grip tightened; her voice filled with empathy. "I understand, Nikki. It's an incredibly difficult situation for everyone involved. But I feel like we're being given a second chance at building a family, a real one. That's something we didn't really experience as children. Lacy being here on Camano, and us finding out she's our sister, is an opportunity for us to show her we're not like Dad and that we actually want her in our lives."

Nikki took a deep breath, her mind grappling with the conflicting emotions that swirled within her. "You're right, Trish. We owe it to Lacy to reach out, to apologize for our initial reaction. We need to show her we're here for her, that we do want to be a part of her life."

Just then, Amy pushed her head through the Star-bucks door to signal them. "Our orders are ready."

The two stepped back into the warm enclosure and walked up to the table Amy had secured for them to take a well-needed coffee break.

As they continued with their shopping, Nikki found herself being drawn into her own thoughts. The guilt and regret she felt about their initial reaction to Lacy's revelation were gnawing at her. Her father's actions had hurt them, but they had hurt Lacy the most—an innocent child who had grown up without a father because of Stuart's selfishness.

Spotting a quaint little shop tucked away in a corner, Nikki could see unique handmade crafts and trinkets adorning the window display. A sign above the entrance read: The Artful Trinket. "This place looks interesting," she commented, gesturing toward the store.

"Oh yeah," Trish responded. "It's owned by Sally. She's...interesting," she finished with a slight upturn of her pursed lips as her brows slightly arched.

"Let's have a look inside," Nikki suggested.

The three women stepped inside, the sound of a bell chiming above their heads. The air was scented with warm cinnamon and vanilla and the aisles filled with rows of interesting pieces.

"Welcome to The Artful Trinket," a woman in a floral dress that seemed to float around her as she approached them greeted. Her brown hair was a mass of wild curls on top of her head and her bright-red lips seemed to compete with her dress, trying to outshine each other.

"Hi, Sally," Trish greeted with a slight smile.

"Oh, Trish, it's so lovely to see you again." Sally quickly reached over and hugged her before blowing an air kiss at the side of her face.

"It's great seeing you too," Trish replied. "This is my sister, Nikki, and my daughter, Amy," she introduced when they separated.

Sally turned to the women with a friendly smile. "It is a pleasure to finally meet you both," she said before pulling them into hugs.

"Hello," Nikki replied politely, as she cast a questioning glance toward her sister.

"I told Trish nearly a year ago that she would have the

most important people, who she had been forced to give up, returning to her life and here you both are," Sally spoke as if reading Nikki's mind. "Although, it seems one is missing," she said with a frown.

Nikki's brows drew together as she looked at the woman with a troubled expression. "And how did you know that?" she asked.

"I am a clairvoyant," Sally said with a confident smile.

"Okay," Nikki spoke slowly, her tone skeptical.

"I can tell that you're seeking answers about someone who has disappointed you throughout your life, but he is no longer here. I can tell you what you seek," the woman offered with a beguiling smile.

"Sally, I wish we had the time, but we need to get going soon," Trish interrupted, breaking whatever spell had compelled Nikki to want to accept the woman's offer.

"Another time then," Sally replied, her smile still in place.

"That was interesting," Amy said, as soon as they left the store. Nikki nodded in agreement before turning her attention to her sister.

"That's Sally for you. She can be a little intense," Trish replied.

"Yeah," Nikki responded as she pondered their interaction with the woman. Determined blue eyes turned to her sister. "I think we need to go see Lacy."

"Yes. I was thinking the same thing," Trish agreed. "Let's go tomorrow."

Nikki nodded.

Chapter Seventeen

Lacy

The wind whispered through the bare skeletons of the trees, stirring the fallen snow into a spectral ballet. The world was polished to a blinding white, a stark contrast to the brooding, overcast sky above. The early morning sun was valiantly struggling to pierce through the heavy curtain of clouds, casting long, ghostly shadows on the pristine landscape. A small firepit crackled and popped, the flames dancing erratically, throwing off a comforting warmth that kept the biting cold at bay.

Lacy was huddled on the porch, wrapped in a thick, faded blanket, her brown eyes reflecting the flickering flames. A steaming cup of coffee sat forgotten on the floor, the warmth seeping into the wooden planks beneath. Her mind was a turbulent whirlpool of emotions, thoughts, and memories.

The revelation to Nikki and Trish still echoed in her ears, their faces contorted in disbelief and denial. The sting of their rejection was a raw, gaping wound in her heart. She had hoped for understanding, acceptance, but all she had received was animosity and rejection. The disappointment was a bitter pill to swallow.

Her gaze drifted to the windows of the house, the soft, yellow light spilling out onto the snow-covered yard. Inside, her children were sleeping, oblivious to their mother's quiet turmoil. David, her seventeen-year-old son, was probably curled up under his blanket, his face peaceful in slumber, a stark contrast to the resentment he harbored toward her.

Lacy missed her husband and her mother. She yearned for their comforting presence, their understanding, and their unconditional love. They were her pillars of strength, her beacons in a stormy sea. With them around, she felt less alone, and their love blunted the harsh edges of life's trials.

She closed her eyes, the memories washing over her like a tidal wave. The sound of her mother's laughter, the warmth of her husband's embrace, the look of pure joy on David's face when he was just a child. A single tear trickled down her cheek, the cold air making it sting like a tiny icicle.

"I'm sorry," she whispered to the icy morning air, her voice barely audible over the crackling fire. "I'm sorry for taking you away from everything you've ever known. I'm sorry for the anger, the resentment, the confusion."

She opened her eyes, staring into the dancing flames. "But I had to. I had to start anew, for all of us. I had to find a place where we could be safe, where we could heal, where we could grow."

She clenched her jaw, determination flashing in her eyes. "I won't let this break me. I won't let this break us. We may be alone, but we have each other. And that's all that matters."

With a deep, steadying breath, she pushed herself off the porch, the blanket falling from her shoulders. She had a new day to face, a new battle to fight, and she would do it with the strength and resilience she had always known.

"I will make this work," she murmured. "For them, for me, for us."

As she headed toward the front door, the crunch of boots on the snow caught her attention. Turning, she saw Phillip. His broad shoulders were covered by a parka and a woolen hat covered his hair. His rugged face was etched with concern as he approached, his breath fogging in the chilly morning air. "Hi, Lacy."

"Phillip," she greeted, her voice a mere whisper against the wind. "What brings you here?"

He shrugged; his gloved hands buried deep into his pockets. "You weren't answering your phone. Just wanted to check if everything's all right."

Lacy managed a weak smile. "I'm fine," she murmured, her gaze drifting back to the firepit.

Phillip studied her for a moment, his eyes softening. "You don't look fine, Lacy."

His words hung in the air, as heavy as the snow-laden clouds above them. Lacy clenched her jaw, the sting of her sisters' rejection flaring anew. His words were gentle, but they pierced her defenses like a well-aimed arrow.

"I'm fine, Phillip," she reiterated, a hint of steel entering her voice. A silence stretched between them, like a chasm too wide to cross.

Phillip sighed, his breath a visible plume in the cold

air. "All right," he said quietly. "If you ever want to talk, I'm here."

She nodded, fighting back unshed tears. "I appreciate that, Phillip."

He gave her a small, sad smile before turning to leave. "Merry Christmas when it comes," he said, his voice carrying over his shoulder.

"Merry Christmas to you too, Phillip," she replied, her voice barely audible.

As she watched his retreating figure, a sigh escaped her lips. It was filled with so much—longing, regret, disappointment. But most of all, it was a sigh of profound loneliness.

With Phillip's departure, the world seemed to fall back into silence. The only sounds were the crackling of the fire and the occasional whisper of the winter wind. She turned and entered the house. Inside the house, she was surprised to find David already up and behind the stove frying what smelled like bacon. Maria was busy setting place mats around the island. Her small hands carefully placed the cutlery.

"What's going on here?" Lacy asked.

David looked over his shoulder with a sheepish grin. "We noticed you looked tired, so we just wanted to do something nice for you," he explained.

Lacy's eyes widened in surprise before she fixed her expression. "That's really sweet of you guys." She smiled.

"Mom, you can go relax in the living room. We'll call you when we're done," Maria instructed.

"Are you guys really kicking me out of my own kitchen?" Lacy asked in mock offence, her hand over her chest.

"Think of it as we're giving you a day off from mom duties," David replied.

"Well, I won't argue with that," Lacy smiled at her children. "Thank you, guys, for this. I appreciate it."

On her way to the living room, the doorbell rang, its chime echoing in the quiet house. Walking to the door, she opened it. On her doorstep stood Nikki and Trish, their faces a mix of regret and hope.

"Nikki, Trish, what are you guys doing here?"

Nikki was the first to speak, her voice barely a whisper, "Hi, Lacy. Can we come in?"

Lacy was taken aback, her heart pounding in her chest, even as she allowed them inside and led them to the living room. She glanced over her shoulder toward her children as she passed the kitchen, where David was flipping an omelet with practiced ease. Maria peeked around her brother; her bright eyes filled with curiosity.

"So, what brought you here?" she asked, when they finally settled in the living room, keeping her expression guarded.

"We wanted to apologize, Lacy," Nikki began, her voice shaking slightly. "Our initial reaction was uncalled for. We were shocked, and we didn't handle it well."

"Nelly told us everything," Trish chimed in. "We want to make it right."

Silence hung heavy between them, punctuated only by the distant sound of David flipping pancakes. Lacy felt a surge of relief, but also apprehension. They were reaching out, yes, but the question was, should she reach back?

"Would you come over for Christmas dinner?"

Lacy hesitated. Her children were here, already

adjusting to so many changes. Could she risk them being disappointed if things didn't work out?

"I appreciate the gesture," Lacy finally said, turning back to her sisters, "but I can't. It's too soon, and I don't want my children to get hurt if things don't work out."

Understanding dawned on Nikki and Trish's faces. They nodded, their expressions reflecting a mix of disappointment and acceptance. "We understand, Lacy," Nikki said softly, "whenever you're ready."

With that, Lacy walked them to the door and as they got into their car and left. She closed the door, leaning against it as a wave of emotion washed over her. She returned to the kitchen, the warm aroma of breakfast wafting through the air. David was at the stove, his brows furrowed in concentration as he flipped a pancake. Maria was perched on a stool, her small fingers playing with the silverware.

David turned as Lacy entered, his face mirroring the concern that had etched lines into her own. "Mom, what's going on?" he asked, his voice betraying a hint of worry.

Lacy took a deep breath, steadying herself. "David, Maria," she began, her voice shaky, "there's something I need to tell you."

Her children looked up at her, their eyes round with concern. "What is it, Mom?" David asked, his spatula still in hand.

"Nikki and Trish... they're my sisters. Your aunts," Lacy blurted out, watching as their expressions shifted from shock to confusion.

David was the first to recover. "What? Why didn't we know about this?" he asked, his confusion giving way to curiosity and possibly frustration.

Lacy sighed, her gaze settling on the worn kitchen

table. "I know I should have said something sooner. I knew I had sisters for a while but I didn't know who they were, let alone that they lived here on the island. I just found out that they are my sisters..." Lacy took in a deep breath before releasing it and continuing, "The truth is, I didn't have a father because he already had another family. I was... I was a secret."

The room fell into a heavy silence, broken only by the sizzle of the frying pan. David's expression softened, his hand coming to rest on his mother's shoulder. "Why didn't you tell us?"

Lacy's eyes dropped to her folded hands on the counter. "I didn't want to burden you with all of this. I wasn't even planning on finding them, and I didn't know they lived on the island. I just wanted us to leave the past behind."

"It's okay. We understand." David gave her a reassuring smile.

"What do... should I call them Aunt Nikki and Aunt Trish?" Maria asked, looking expectantly at her mother.

"Um. I don't know yet. How do you feel about calling them aunts?" Lacy asked.

Maria seemed to ponder the question before innocent brown eyes looked up at Lacy with a mixture of hope and anticipation. "I think I'd like that," she spoked softly.

"Okay, sweetie," Lacy smiled encouragingly. As if sensing their question she answered, "They invited us to have Christmas dinner with them and the rest of the family...but we're not going."

"Mom, I think you should go to the dinner," David said, his voice firm. "Get to know them. We can handle it."

Lacy looked up at her son, surprise flickering in her eyes. "David, I..."

154

"I know it's hard," he interrupted, his gaze steady. "But we're stronger than you think. We're your family too."

Lacy felt a lump in her throat, her eyes filling with tears. "All right, David," she managed, her voice choked with emotion. "I'll think about it."

As she looked at her children, Lacy felt a glimmer of hope. Despite the storm they were in, they were still together, still strong. Maybe, just maybe, they could weather this storm and come out stronger on the other side.

Christmas morning dawned bright and clear, the snow sparkling under the bright winter sun. "Guys, come on downstairs. It's Christmas!" Lacy called up to her children. David and Maria emerged at the top of the stairs, wiping the sleep from their eyes.

"I made hot chocolate with the little marshmallows you guys love so much and sticky buns," she told them when they came down the stairs. "They're in the living room."

"Mom, couldn't this have waited until the sun was out? I'm still tired," David grumbled, even as he walked past her toward the living room. Maria gave her a small smile before following him, Lacy walking behind them. Their faces lit up at the sight of the small pile of gifts under the Christmas tree.

"When did you get all these?" David asked, grabbing a cup of hot chocolate and a sticky bun before plopping down on the plush rug the tree sat on.

"I got them a couple of weeks ago, actually, but I thought it would be a nice surprise if you didn't see them until today," Lacy smiled, as she took a seat beside her children on the rug.

Maria held up a neatly wrapped gift with her name

on it and a wide smile lifted her lips. "Can I open this?" she turned and asked Lacy.

Lacy smiled encouragingly. "Of course. It's yours."

Maria carefully tore off the wrapping and a gasp fell from her lips. Her eyes flew to her mother's smiling face. "How did you know that I wanted this?" she asked, still in disbelief.

"You're my little Picasso. I've always known," Lacy said.

"Thanks, Mom," Maria replied, rising on her knees and reaching over to hug her mother.

"You're welcome, sweetie." Lacy smiled against her hair; happy she had been able to get the deluxe art set she knew her daughter had wanted for some time now.

It was David's turn to open his present. His brows furrowed over his green eyes that stared in confusion at her as he held the car safety kit in his hands. "I don't get it," he said.

Lacy smiled. "That is a car safety kit."

"But I don't have a car," David replied.

"Don't you?" Her smile grew as she gave him a small box with a bow on top. David slowly reached for it and took his time opening it, as if afraid it would not be what he expected.

"You got me a car?" he whispered in awe. Lacy nodded. "Oh...what?" He flew up and excitedly held up the key fob. "Mom, this is...wow. Thank you," he said, embracing her.

A smile lifted the corners of her mouth. It had been so long since she and her son had shared a hug, and it felt like coming home. "You're welcome, sweetie."

As they continued to exchange more gifts and shared warm embraces, Lacy still noticed the unspoken longing in their eyes. The day was always bittersweet, reminding them of the one person who was missing, Carlos. The smiles became a little strained, the joy tinged with a touch of melancholy.

"I love you both so much," Lacy told them, pulling them into a tight hug. "Your father would be so proud of you." In that moment, she made a decision. She didn't want this Christmas to be shadowed by loss and regret. She wanted it to be a day of new beginnings, of healing, and of love.

With a resolute nod, she said, "I've decided we're going to that Christmas dinner."

The surprise on their faces was quickly replaced by understanding. They nodded, David giving her a small smile, Maria's eyes sparkling with anticipation.

Chapter Eighteen

Nikki

The first rays of the winter sun had barely peeked over the horizon, bathing the room in the soft glow of Christmas light. Nikki felt a weight bounce onto her bed. Her eyes fluttered open to find Amy, beaming down at her in the soft morning light, her blue eyes wide with excitement.

"Merry Christmas, Aunt Nikki!" she squealed, her excitement making the room seem brighter. Her blond hair was a messy halo around her head, and her eyes sparkled with holiday cheer.

Nikki let out a groggy laugh. "Merry Christmas, Amy," she replied. "You sure know how to wake someone up with a bang."

"Come to the living room. I have something planned for you guys," Amy instructed before waltzing out of the room.

Rubbing the sleep out of her eyes, Nikki slipped out of bed and padded down the hallway. The scent of cinnamon and warm chocolate wafted through the house, mingling with the smell of pine from the Christmas tree. As she moved toward the living room, she found Trish, clad in her festive Christmas pajamas, looking out the window at the snow-covered neighborhood.

"Did Amy bombard you too?" Trish asked without turning around, her voice soft, a hint of a smile dancing on her lips.

Nikki chuckled, shaking her head. "Oh, yeah. How long has she been up?" she questioned.

"I'm going to guess before dawn."

Just then, Amy burst into the room, her cheeks flushed from the warmth of the kitchen. A tray of steaming hot chocolate and a plate stacked high with gooey cinnamon rolls balanced in her hands filled the room with their enticing aroma.

"Hot chocolate and cinnamon rolls, fresh from the oven!" she exclaimed, her voice filled with excitement. "It's the perfect Christmas breakfast."

"You're as giddy as a child on her first Christmas, Amy," Nikki teased, accepting a mug of hot chocolate and sinking into the plush sofa.

Trish's eyes momentarily clouded over, a poignant look crossing her face. Nikki could guess her thoughts—the twenty-one Christmases she'd missed with her daughter. Trish had never gotten the chance to celebrate this joyous day with Amy before—the weight of that loss was a burden she carried in her heart—another thing their father had taken away from them. But before Nikki could say anything, Amy sensed the heaviness in the room and spoke up.

"You know, Mom, I'm really glad we get to spend Christmas together. We're making new memories as a family, and that's pretty special."

Trish's eyes brightened, a tremulous smile tugging at the corners of her lips. "You're absolutely right, sweetheart. And I'm so glad we get to make some new ones this year. I wouldn't trade this moment for anything."

Once they finished their breakfast, the trio gathered under the twinkling Christmas tree, the fire crackling warmly in the fireplace. The room was filled with the rustle of wrapping paper and soft laughter as they exchanged gifts.

Nikki handed Amy a beautifully wrapped package. Inside were new baking tools for her pastry class. Amy's eyes lit up like the Christmas lights around them. "These are all brands!" Amy exclaimed, her eyes wide with excitement. "Thanks, Aunt Nikki. I really appreciate this."

"You're welcome, sweetie." Nikki smiled broadly.

"Your turn." Amy smiled, handing her a present.

Nikki raised a brow as she accepted the present. Carefully, she tore off the wrapping to reveal a leather-bound journal engraved with her initials. "Oh, Amy, this is perfect. Thank you so much."

"You're welcome," Amy smiled. "Mom, this one's for you." She turned to Trish and handed her a large wrapped package.

"Oh, Amy this is perfect," Trish beamed with gratitude and pride when she removed the wrapper to reveal a photo album with the inscription *Making New Memories* on the front.

"Open it," Amy urged. Trish flipped the cover to find

a large photo of them at the Humane Society smiling at the camera.

"I love it," Trish spoke with feeling before opening her arms to hug her daughter tightly, as a few tears moistened the corners of her eyes. "This is for you." She handed Amy a small, wrapped box.

Trish's gift to Amy was a delicate necklace, the locket big enough to hold their pictures. As Amy opened it, her eyes welled up with unshed tears.

"I love it, Mom," she whispered, her voice choked with emotion.

Their laughter and warmth filled the room, echoes of past Christmases merging with the joy of the present, painting a beautiful picture of love, family, and the magic of Christmas.

After their sweet moments and breakfast, the three women busied themselves in the kitchen, preparing for the feast they would be having with their family and friends a little later. Trish left two hours later to help Kaylyn in organizing for the Christmas dinner the remaining guests would be having.

"All right, the table is set for a party of seven. We just need to add the finishing touches." Amy stood back from the table, admiring the arrangement. The warm glow of Christmas lights filled the cozy dining room, casting an enchanting aura as the soft melody of holiday music filled the air, weaving a tapestry of joy and nostalgia that enveloped the room. Outside, delicate snowflakes danced gracefully from the heavens, blanketing the landscape in a shimmering white. "Are you sure Lacy won't change her mind?" she asked, casting hopeful eyes at her aunt.

"I'm sure," Nikki affirmed with a sad smile. "She was

pretty clear she needed to spend this time with her children."

"That's a bummer. I really wanted to get to know them."

"Hopefully, some other time," Nikki replied, although her tone held a hint of uncertainty.

The two continued to work on the setup for the dinner. With meticulous care, Nikki arranged the silverware, ensuring each piece was perfectly aligned. Amy, her hands delicately placed vibrant red poinsettias in the center of the table, their velvety petals adding a pop of color against the crisp white tablecloth. Nikki stepped back to admire their handiwork, a smile of satisfaction tugging at the corners of her lips.

"Yup. We're definitely in business for today's showdown," Nikki nodded approvingly. "Let me go check on the ham, it's just about ready to be removed from the oven."

"I need to add some whipped cream to the pies," Amy said. The two headed for the kitchen to finish prepping the meal.

An hour later, and Nikki and Amy were putting the finishing touches on the meal. The jingling sound of the chimes at the front door signaled Trish's arrival. Nikki walked to the front door to meet her.

"Gosh, it's super cold out today." Trish shivered as a gust of frosty air rushed through the opened door.

"You're right. It's really cold out there." Nikki shivered, rubbing her arms as she stared out at the snow blanketing the driveway. It looked a lot thicker, like an inch of snow was now covering the ground. "I hope the guys can travel through this snow." She worried her bottom lip.

Trish closed the door and shrugged out of her coat.

"It's not that bad. They'll be able to make it," she assured Nikki. "It's early January we have to worry about."

Nikki gave her a questioning look.

"We get snowstorms around that time," Trish explained.

"You know the seasons here better than I do, so I'm counting on that."

As the clock ticked closer to the much-anticipated dinnertime, the doorbell rang.

"I'll get it," Amy volunteered, already heading for the front door.

"It sure smells great in here," came Paul's voice as he, Sarah, and Aaron entered the living room.

"Merry Christmas, everyone," Sarah spoke excitedly.

After sharing a brief but affectionate embrace with her fiancé, Nikki turned to Sarah. "Hi, Sarah, Aaron, I'm glad you could make it."

"Thank you." Aaron nodded with a smile on his lips.

"Hi, Nikki. We're glad to be here too.' Sarah smiled affectionately.

"How's the little one?" Nikki asked, staring pointedly at Sarah's baby bump visibly rounding beneath her festive sweater.

"She's great," Sarah replied before making a face as she added, "She's great and thriving but hardly gives me time to get work done."

Nikki smiled knowingly. "I know it might feel foreign to have so much free time on your hands, but it is a good thing for you and the baby."

"That's what I've been telling her," Aaron expressed.

Sarah sighed. "I know."

Nikki reached over and placed her hand on Sarah's

forearm. "Enjoy the free time. You're gonna need it when she comes."

"Thank you. I'll try." Sarah smiled appreciatively.

Nikki caught Paul's loving gaze and she smiled at him.

"Do you need any help setting the table?" she heard Sarah ask Amy.

"No, no, Sarah," Amy chided gently, her eyes filled with maternal care. "You shouldn't be exerting yourself. You need to take it easy for the baby's sake."

Sarah nodded understandingly, her hand instinctively resting on her round belly as she smiled gratefully. "I know, Amy. I just wanted to help a little."

Amy's smile softened, and she placed a reassuring hand on Sarah's arm. "We appreciate the gesture, but we want you to be safe and comfortable. Let us take care of everything tonight. Your health and the baby's well-being are our top priority."

The doorbell rang again. It was Reed who had arrived and Nelly right behind him.

"Merry Christmas, everyone. What did I miss?" he asked, his warm smile lighting up the room. He was closely followed by Nelly, who exuded holiday cheer in every step and had a mischievous twinkle in her eyes.

Trish's eyes met Reed's, and an affectionate smile blossomed on her lips. "Hi," she greeted him.

"Hi," Reed returned with an equally emanating smile as she walked over to him by the doorway.

"Mom," Amy called out to get Trish's attention. Trish turned to look at her and Amy's eyes lifted upward, causing Trish to do the same. Above their heads hung a mistletoe.

"Darn it. I was hoping I would have been the one

under there with this young strapping man," Nelly spoke in a disappointed voice, although her eyes twinkled with mischief.

The room erupted in laughter as Trish buried her face in Reed's chest.

"Don't worry, Nelly. You'll get your kiss before the day ends," Paul reassured her.

"Ah, a man after my own heart." The room erupted in laughter once more before everyone turned expectant gazes toward Reed and Trish.

Underneath the mistletoe hanging in the doorway, Trish and Reed shared a sweet kiss, eliciting a chorus of "aahs" from the room and playful laughter following.

"Come on, Nikki, your turn!" Paul urged with a mischievous twinkle in his eye, nudging Nikki playfully.

Nikki chuckled, shaking her head, her cheeks flushed with a mixture of amusement and affection. "We're not standing under the mistletoe, Paul."

But to everyone's surprise, Paul produced a sprig of mistletoe from his pocket and raised it over their heads with a sheepish grin. The room erupted into laughter, the sound like tinkling bells, and Nikki couldn't help but feel the warmth of Paul's love embrace her completely.

"So, you've just been walking around with mistletoe in your pocket, huh?" Nikki teased, raising an eyebrow at Paul's preparedness.

Paul chuckled, his eyes twinkling mischievously. "For you, my dear, I am always prepared," he replied with a smirk. Nikki's laughter bubbled up from deep within her, her heart fluttering with warmth and affection. With a shared glance and hearts brimming with love, Nikki and Paul leaned in, closing the gap between them, and shared a tender kiss under the impromptu mistletoe, the moment filled with the magic and enchantment of the season.

Yet, despite the joyous gathering and the love that filled the room, there lingered a sense of incompleteness in the air, a palpable absence that weighed on Nikki's heart. She couldn't shake the feeling of incompleteness. Although she had only known Lacy under a month, she missed her being here... with family.

However, as the family settled in around the table in the dining room, passing around plates filled with scrumptious food and exchanging lively conversation, the feeling dissipated for a moment.

The doorbell rang, interrupting the quiet hum of laughter and stories being shared.

"Are we expecting anyone else?" Trish asked.

Nikki's heart skipped a beat. "No. Everyone's here," she replied before rising from her seat. Anticipation coursed through her veins, as she hurriedly made her way to the door.

She swung the door open, her eyes widening in surprise and delight. Standing on the threshold was Lacy and her two children.

"Lacy," Nikki breathed, her voice thick with emotion. "You're here."

Lacy, her eyes shimmering with a mixture of hope and uncertainty, stepped forward tentatively, her smile widening as she caught sight of Nikki's warm embrace. "I hope it's not too late to join you," she said softly, her voice tinged with vulnerability.

"Of course not. I was hoping you would show up." As Lacy and her children stepped inside and shrugged out of their coats, Nikki's heart swelled with emotion as she reached out and enveloped Lacy in a tight embrace, "You're always welcome here, among family."

Lacy's eyes brimmed with tears, a tearful smile gracing her lips. "Thanks, Nikki. I appreciate that."

Nikki smiled reassuringly. "Let's go meet the others."

Lacy stepped farther into the warmth of Nikki's home, her children following closely behind as they made their way down the hall.

"Look who's here," Nikki joyfully announced.

All eyes turned to them then and Trish quickly rose from her seat, her eyes filled with relief and happiness.

"Oh, Lacy. You're here." She walked over and pulled her sister into a tight hug. "I'm glad you changed your mind."

"Me too," Lacy spoke with feeling.

"Welcome, Lacy. We're happy you're here."

As Lacy and her children joined the table and conversation, all of them gathered around the table, united as a family at last, the sense of completeness settled over the room like a comforting blanket. The missing piece had been found, and together, they would celebrate this Christmas with a renewed sense of love, forgiveness, and belonging.

Chapter Nineteen

Lacy

As the clock struck half past eleven, Lacy, David, and Maria hurried into the cozy living room, their breath billowing in the frosty air. The crackling fire from the nearby fireplace illuminated the porch behind them, casting dancing shadows across the walls of their homey abode. The twinkling lights of the Christmas tree in the corner infused the room with a warm, festive glow.

"Mom, can we talk for a moment?" David asked, a hint of anticipation in his voice as he glanced at his mother, his eyes reflecting the flickering lights of the tree.

Lacy smiled at her son, her heart swelling with love for her children. "Of course, David. What's on your mind?" she replied, settling onto the plush sofa, the soft crackling of the fire providing a comforting backdrop to their conversation.

David hesitated for a moment, his gaze flitting between his sister, Maria, who was snuggled up in a blanket on the adjacent armchair, and his mother. "Well, I was thinking..." he began, his words trailing off as he searched for the right way to express himself. "I've been thinking a lot about everything lately," he repeated, his voice tinged with a mix of sadness and determination. "About us moving to Camano Island and leaving everything behind in Santa Monica."

Lacy listened intently, her heart aching for her son as he spoke. "I understand, David," she said softly, her eyes meeting his. "It's been a big adjustment for all of us, and I know it hasn't been easy, especially for you."

David nodded, his shoulders slumping slightly as he continued, "I know we didn't have a choice, Mom. But I was just so angry. I had so much to count on back in Santa Monica—my friends, my swim team, the house we've lived in all my life. It felt like I was leaving behind a piece of Dad, you know? Like I was losing a part of him all over again."

Lacy reached out and took her son's hand, offering him the comfort of her touch. "I understand, sweetheart. It's okay to feel that way," she reassured him, her voice filled with empathy. "Leaving behind the familiar and the memories we shared there—it's natural to grieve for what we've lost."

David took a deep breath, the weight of his emotions evident in his eyes. "I've been acting out, and I'm sorry. I promise to do better," he said, his voice filled with sincerity. "I just miss Dad, and I miss how things used to be."

Lacy's heart ached at her son's words. She knew David had been struggling with their father's absence, especially during the holiday season. "I miss him too, sweetheart," she murmured, her voice filled with empathy. "Your father was a wonderful man, and he would be so proud of the person you're becoming."

Maria, who had been listening quietly, spoke up, her eyes shimmering with unshed tears. "I miss his jokes," she admitted, her voice soft and wistful. "He made everything so much fun."

Lacy's lips slightly curved upward. "Your father loved Christmas. He always used to tell the silliest jokes while we watched the countdown. Like, why don't skeletons like Christmas?"

"I know this one," David responded. "Because it rattles their bones."

The three erupted in laughs and giggles.

"I've got one," Maria chimed in. "Why did the fireworks go to school on Christmas?"

"Oh, I know this one," Lacy jumped up. She tapped her chin as she tried to remember. When it finally came back to her, a twinkle shone in her brown eyes. "Because it wanted to be a little brighter," she spoke triumphantly.

Again, there were laughs and giggles and they continued to go through Carlos's corny jokes.

Lacy enveloped her children in a warm embrace, holding them close as they shared memories of their father. "Your dad may not be here with us, but he's always in our hearts," she said, her voice gentle but resolute. "We'll keep his spirit alive by celebrating the love and joy he brought into our lives."

As they sat together, sharing stories of Christmas and memories, the faint, distant crackling of the fire echoed through. The warmth of the fire, the soft glow of the Christmas tree, and the love that enveloped them filled the room with a sense of peace and togetherness.

In that moment, Lacy knew that their bond as a family would carry them through any hardship, and she felt grateful for the love and strength they found in each other.

As the clock struck midnight, the room erupted in cheers and the soft crackling of fireworks outside. Lacy pulled her children into her arms to share a warm embrace before pulling away, a glimmer of hope in her eyes. "Merry Christmas, David," Lacy said, a small smile playing on her lips.

David returned the smile. "Merry Christmas, Mom," he replied.

"Merry Christmas," Maria echoed.

"May we all have the happiness we deserve," Lacy added.

In that intimate moment, surrounded by the echoes of celebration, they found solace in their shared connection and the unbreakable bond of family.

* * *

The morning sun kissed the horizon as the day unfolded after New Year's Day. Lacy felt a mix of anticipation and unease as she awaited Phillip's arrival to finish the electrical work. She greeted him at the door with a hesitant smile. "Happy New Year, Phillip."

He returned her greeting with a warm smile of his own. "Happy New Year, Lacy." His breath misted in the chilly air. "How are you doing?"

Lacy's nerves danced beneath her skin as she let out a small chuckle. "Oh, you know, just trying to start the year off right."

Phillip nodded in understanding. "Well, let's get this

breaker box sorted out. I remember suggesting we install a new one when I came last time, but you preferred to stick with the old one."

Lacy's eyes cast downward as she sheepishly replied, "Yeah, I should have listened to you. You're the expert after all. The old one has been causing us so many issues."

A sense of satisfaction glimmered in Phillip's eyes. "It's never too late to make a change, Lacy. I'm glad we're doing the right thing now."

As Phillip got to work on installing the new breaker box, Lacy watched in admiration as David joined him, offering assistance without hesitation. It was a marked change from their previous interactions, and Lacy marveled at her son's growth and maturity.

"Hey, Phillip, do you need a hand with anything? I could pass you the tools or help you with the wiring," David asked, his voice filled with genuine warmth.

Phillip grinned, grateful for the newfound camaraderie. "I appreciate the offer, David. Having an extra set of hands would definitely speed things up. Thank you."

Lacy observed them work together, a mixture of pride and hope swelling within her. It seemed David was slowly but surely coming around, the protective barrier he had built around his father's memories, where he refused to be nice to any male figure who came around them, was gradually softening.

Once the task was completed, the air in the room took on a heavy, uncertain quality. Phillip's expression grew more serious as he approached Lacy, his brow furrowed with concern. "Lacy, can we talk?"

She nodded, her heart fluttering with anticipation as she led him to the living room, seeking the privacy they needed. "Of course. Take a seat, if you'd like."

Phillip shook his head, declining her offer. Instead, he chose to stand, his hands tucked into the pockets of his jeans as he shifted his weight from one foot to the other. The nervous energy radiating from him only heightened Lacy's curiosity and anxiety. She braced herself for his words.

"I have to ask... Have I done something wrong? I've noticed you've been distant lately," he said, his gray eyes searching her face, hoping to unravel the mystery behind her recent behavior.

Lacy's heart seemed to skip a beat as she processed his question. She swallowed hard, trying to find the right words. "Phillip, I want you to know that it's not you. It's never been about anything you've done. I value our friendship, truly."

His gaze softened as he listened, a flicker of understanding washing over his features. "I appreciate that, Lacy. But something has changed. You've been distant, and I can't help but wonder if it's something I did or said."

Lacy took a deep breath, her hands fidgeting with the seams of her shirt. "It's not about something you did wrong, Phillip. It's about where I am in my life right now. My kids have been through so much these past couple of years, especially David, he's so protective of his father's memories. I'm just not ready for anything serious."

The concern in Phillip's eyes deepened, but his voice remained gentle. "I understand. You're protecting your children, and that's commendable. But, Lacy, I want you to know that I've never wanted to rush into anything serious. I value our friendship too much to jeopardize it."

Lacy met his gaze, her heart aching with a mixture of relief and sadness. "Thank you for understanding, Phillip.

I genuinely appreciate it. But I also worry that I'm not ready for anything more. I'm still healing too."

Phillip nodded; his voice filled with empathy. "Lacy, I want you to know that I'm okay with taking things slow. I cherish our friendship, and I don't want to push you into something you're not ready for. We can navigate this at your pace."

Relief washed over Lacy as she exhaled the breath she had been holding. "Thank you, Phillip. I appreciate your understanding."

A mischievous twinkle danced in Phillip's eyes, and a playful smile curved his lips. "Well, I guess I'll have to put my dreams of a fairy-tale romance on hold then."

Lacy let out a genuine laugh, appreciating the light-heartedness he brought to the moment. "Oh, well. Life rarely goes according to plan, right?"

A mischievous glint gleamed in Phillip's eyes as he playfully nudged her arm. "Well, at least we've got the breaker box sorted out. Guess that's progress, and it went according to plan, right?"

Lacy chuckled, grateful for his lightheartedness amidst the weighty conversation. "Yes, I suppose it is. And hey, at least we make a pretty good team when it comes to electrical work."

Their laughter filled the room, permeating the air with a sense of joy and ease. In that moment, Lacy realized, even though the road ahead might be uncertain, she had a friend by her side, willing to support her regardless of the direction they took.

"I told Trish and Nikki that they were my sisters," she confessed to Phillip as they had settled into a comfortable silence.

"Really?" Phillip's eyes widened in surprise. "How did that go?"

"Well, at first, they didn't believe me but then they did their research and found out it was true," Lacy explained. "The day you came here, I was still reeling from them not believing me and I took it out on you. I'm sorry." She gave him an apologetic look.

"That's okay. I understand, you were hurting," he assured her. "So, how is the relationship now?"

"We're...we're learning to navigate this new relationship," Lacy expressed. "Me and the kids had Christmas dinner with them and we've spoken a few times on the phone.

"That's great, Lacy. I'm happy for you," Phillip expressed.

Lacy's lips turned up into a smile. "It really does feel like everything is falling into place," she expressed.

As they walked back toward David, ready to bid farewell to Phillip, Lacy couldn't help but feel a renewed sense of hope. Maybe, just maybe, they could navigate this delicate dance of friendship amidst her lingering past.

David's eyes widened in curiosity as they approached. "Everything okay, Mom?"

Lacy nodded, her heart swelling with pride. "Everything's great, David. Just making sure everything went smoothly. And it looks like it did, thanks to both of you."

David beamed with satisfaction, wariness flowing out of him. "Well, Phillip did most of the work. I just helped a little."

Phillip clapped him on the back with a chuckle. "Don't downplay yourself, David. You were a huge help. We make quite the team, don't we?"

They all chuckled, relishing in the newfound connection they had formed. The awkwardness of earlier had been swept away, replaced with an understanding and respect that would help guide them through whatever lay ahead.

As the day wore on and the sun cast its golden hue over the horizon, they bid their farewells. Lacy watched as Phillip drove off, feeling a sense of contentment settle within her. Their friendship had withstood the tests and tribulations, and now, they could move forward, hand in hand, navigating the delicate balance of their lives together.

Chapter Twenty

Nikki

As they trudged through the lightly snow-covered trail in the serene Camano Ridge Forest Preserve, the crisp air filled Nikki's lungs, invigorating her senses. The sun peeked through the trees, casting a soft glow on the pristine white landscape, creating a picturesque winter scene.

Nikki turned to Lacy, her breath visible in the chilly air, and smiled. "I'm so glad you agreed to come on this hike with me, Lacy. It's such a peaceful place to clear the mind."

Lacy nodded, her cheeks rosy from the cold. "I'm happy to be here, Nikki. It's beautiful. And it's nice to spend time with you."

As they continued along the trail, the conversation turned to their father. Nikki hesitated for a moment, then took a deep breath before speaking, "You know, Lacy, our father wasn't exactly the perfect dad. He had this idealized image of what he wanted us to be, especially in his career as a journalist. It was like he wanted us to live out his unfulfilled dreams."

Lacy furrowed her brow, a look of curiosity and concern crossing her features. "Did you both become journalists then?"

Nikki chuckled softly, a hint of bitterness in her voice. "Just me," she said. "But I pursued a different kind of journalism than he did. I wanted to make my own mark, not just follow in his footsteps. Trish studied journalism too, but she never ended up working in the field."

Lacy listened intently, her eyes reflecting empathy for Nikki's struggles. "It must have been tough, trying to live up to his expectations," she said, her voice filled with understanding.

Nikki nodded, a wistful expression on her face. "It was. I felt like I was constantly trying to measure up to an impossible standard. It took me a long time to realize I didn't have to live my life for him."

The two sisters walked in silence for a moment, the only sound the crunch of the snow beneath their boots. The weight of Nikki's revelation hung in the air between them, a newfound understanding deepening their bond.

Finally, Lacy spoke, her voice gentle, "I'm sorry you had to go through that, Nikki. But I'm glad you found your own path. You're a strong and independent woman, and I admire that about you."

Nikki smiled gratefully at Lacy. "Thank you, Lacy. And I'm grateful to have you in my life now. It means a lot to me."

They continued their hike, the forest enveloping them in a sense of peace and tranquility. As they walked, their conversation flowed effortlessly, weaving a tapestry of shared experiences and newfound connections, binding them together as sisters in a way neither of them had thought possible.

As they continued their hike through the tranquil winter landscape, Nikki couldn't shake the weight of the recent revelations from her mind. The peaceful surroundings seemed at odds with the turmoil churning within her, but she knew she needed to share the truth with Lacy.

"Lacy, there's something I need to tell you," Nikki began, her voice tinged with a mix of sadness and relief. "Our father, Stuart, convinced Trish to give up her baby when she was only nineteen."

Lacy's eyes widened in shock, the gravity of Nikki's words sinking in. "I had no idea," she murmured, her voice barely above a whisper. "That's awful. I can't imagine how devastating that must have been.

Nikki nodded solemnly. "It's been a long and painful journey for all of us. I wanted to adopt the baby because I'd just found out I couldn't have children and I had been married at the time."

"Oh, wow. You poor thing," Lacy spoke sympathetically.

"It's okay now though. We found Amy, Trish's daughter—your niece—last summer, after twenty-one years. Our family has been broken for so long, and we're only now beginning to come together and heal."

Lacy's brow furrowed with empathy. "That must have been incredibly difficult for all of you," she said softly. "I can't even imagine..."

Nikki took a deep breath, her gaze fixed on the trail ahead. "It's been a roller coaster of emotions, that's for sure. But finding you, Lacy, has been a beacon of light in the darkness. I never thought I'd have another sister, and now that I do, I'm grateful for every moment."

Lacy's eyes glistened with unshed tears. "I'm so happy to have found you too, Nikki... and Trish," she said, her voice trembling with emotion. "I've felt so alone in this world, especially after my mother and husband passed away. It's been a long, lonely road."

Nikki reached out and placed a comforting hand on Lacy's shoulder, offering a wordless gesture of support. "You're not alone anymore, Lacy. You have a family who loves you, and we're here for you, no matter what."

The two sisters walked in silence for a while, the weight of their shared experiences binding them together in a newfound kinship. The forest seemed to embrace them, offering solace and understanding in its quiet embrace.

As they continued their hike, their conversation gradually shifted to lighter topics, the bond between them growing stronger with each step. The beauty of the winter landscape seemed to mirror the hope and healing that blossomed within their hearts, a symbol of new beginnings and the promise of a brighter future.

As they walked along the snow-dusted trail, Nikki felt a newfound sense of purpose welling up inside her. The weight of the past seemed to lift from her shoulders as she turned to Lacy, her eyes filled with determination and hope.

"Lacy, I want you to know that I truly want us to become close," Nikki began, her voice filled with sincerity. "I'm so happy to know that Trish, Amy, and I aren't all there is to our family. I want us to create new memories and forge a bond that's stronger than anything we've experienced before."

Lacy's eyes sparkled with emotion as she met Nikki's gaze. "I would like that," she said, a soft smile playing on her lips. "I've always yearned for a sense of family, especially after everything I've been through. To have sisters by my side means more to me than I can express."

Nikki nodded, a warm feeling spreading through her chest. "We have a chance to build something beautiful together, to support each other, and to create a sense of belonging that we've both been missing for so long."

The forest around them seemed to echo their sentiments, the gentle rustle of the leaves and the distant call of a bird adding a serene backdrop to their conversation. The air was filled with a sense of possibility, as if the world itself was conspiring to bring them closer together.

As they continued their hike, their dialogue flowed effortlessly, weaving a tapestry of shared dreams and the promise of a brighter future. Their laughter mingled with the rustling of the trees, creating a symphony of newfound connection and kinship.

With each step, Nikki and Lacy felt the bonds of sisterhood strengthening, their hearts opening to the possibility of a future filled with love, understanding, and unwavering support. The winter landscape seemed to shimmer with a newfound warmth, mirroring the blossoming relationship between the two sisters as they walked side by side, ready to embrace the journey ahead.

After their invigorating hike through the snow-covered trails, Nikki and Lacy decided to stop at a cozy coffee shop nestled near the forest. The warm, rich aroma of freshly brewed coffee enveloped them as they entered, and the comforting buzz of conversation filled the air.

As they settled into a corner table, sipping their steaming drinks, a familiar figure caught Nikki's eye. It was Nelly, the kind-hearted elderly woman, who often frequented the shop. She waved them over with a warm smile, and they joined her at her table.

"Nikki, Lacy, it's wonderful to see you both," Nelly greeted them, her eyes twinkling with warmth. "How was your hike? The forest is particularly beautiful this time of year, isn't it?"

Nikki smiled gratefully at Nelly's welcoming presence. "It was amazing, Nelly. The snow-covered trails were like something out of a winter wonderland."

Nelly nodded, her gaze turning thoughtful. "Nature has a way of soothing the soul and bringing people together, doesn't it? Speaking of which, how have you two been getting along? You seem to have quite the bond."

Nikki glanced at Lacy, a sense of kinship and understanding passing between them. "We've been getting to know each other, and it's been really special. I'm grateful to have found Lacy, and I feel like we're beginning a new chapter together."

Nelly's eyes softened with understanding. "Family is a precious thing, isn't it? It's never too late to find connections that can enrich our lives."

As they enjoyed their conversation, Lacy's phone suddenly rang, breaking the peaceful ambiance of the coffee shop. Her expression turned to one of concern as she listened intently to the caller on the other end.

"David's school?" Lacy exclaimed, her voice tinged with worry. "I'll be right there. Thank you for letting me know." Once off the phone, she immediately started packing up her belongings.

Nikki placed a comforting hand on Lacy's arm. "Is everything okay, Lacy? Do you need me to come with you?"

Lacy shook her head, a sense of urgency in her movements. "I need to get to David's school quickly. Thank you, Nikki, but I'll manage. I'll see you soon."

With that, Lacy hurriedly made her way out of the coffee shop, leaving Nikki and Nelly at the table, a sense of concern lingering in the air.

Nelly placed a reassuring hand on Nikki's shoulder. "It's moments like these that remind us of the unpredictability of life, isn't it, dear? I have no doubt that Lacy will handle whatever comes her way with the strength I've seen in her."

Nikki nodded, her thoughts with Lacy as she watched her leave. "You're right, Nelly. I just hope everything turns out okay for her and David."

As the conversation continued, Nikki couldn't shake the worry from her mind, but she found comfort in Nelly's wisdom and the warmth of the coffee shop around her. The world outside may have been uncertain, but in that moment, she felt a sense of peace and camaraderie, knowing that she had found a new friend in Nelly and a newfound sister in Lacy.

Chapter Twenty-One

Nikki

As the February wedding date rapidly approached, Nikki found herself in a whirlwind of activity. Her days were a frenzy of appointments with florists, caterers, and dress fittings, all in a bid to ensure that her special day would be perfect. Trish, her ever-efficient sister, and Amy, her bubbly and creative niece, had taken on the role of her unofficial wedding planners at Nikki's insistence. They had plunged into the task with gusto, carefully managing the growing list of tasks and vendors as they sought to fulfill Nikki's vision for a personal and intimate celebration.

"Okay, so we've got the seating arrangements sorted for the reception, and the florist is all set for the centerpieces," Trish said, tapping her pen against the clipboard as she and Amy sat with Nikki in her cozy living room. "What's next on the agenda, bride-to-be?"

Nikki let out a sigh, her brows furrowed with concern. "I just can't believe how big this guest list has gotten. I wanted something small and intimate, and now we're over seventy people. How did this happen?"

Amy reached over to pat Nikki's hand reassuringly. "It's okay, Aunt Nikki. You're just too well-loved. Everyone wants to be there to celebrate with you and Paul."

Nikki managed a small smile at her niece before turning her attention back to Trish. "I know, but I wanted to keep it intimate. I don't want it to feel like a big production. I want it to be personal, you know?"

Trish nodded understandingly. "I get it, Nik. But at this point, it's going to be hard to trim down the guest list without hurting anyone's feelings. Maybe we can focus on making the event feel intimate in other ways, like the decor and the overall ambiance."

Nikki sighed, feeling torn between her desire for intimacy and the reality of the situation. "You're right, Trish. I just... I want everything to be perfect."

Amy perked up, her eyes sparkling with excitement. "Well, how about we focus on the little details? Like personalized favors for the guests, or a special touch for the ceremony? We can make those moments really meaningful and personal."

Nikki's eyes lit up at the suggestion. "That's a great idea, Amy. I love the thought of adding those personal touches. It will make the day feel special for everyone, no matter how many people are there."

The three women fell into animated discussion, brainstorming ideas for personalized touches that would infuse the wedding with warmth and intimacy. As they talked, Nikki felt a renewed sense of excitement and purpose, knowing that even with a larger guest list, she could still create the personal and meaningful celebration she had always envisioned. With the support of her sister and niece, she was confident her wedding would be a day to remember for all the right reasons.

"That's a fantastic idea, Trish!" Nikki exclaimed, her eyes brightening with enthusiasm. "The inn's backyard is so lovely, and it has that cozy, intimate feel I've been dreaming of. Plus, it's just a short drive from our house."

Trish nodded, a satisfied smile spreading across her face. "Exactly! And I've heard they have these beautiful, twinkling string lights that we can use to create a magical atmosphere. It'll be like a fairy-tale winter wonderland."

Amy clapped her hands together. "Oh, that sounds amazing! We could have a hot chocolate and mulled wine station too, to keep everyone warm and toasty."

Nikki's excitement grew as she imagined the scene unfolding. "Yes, and we can set up a roaring firepit with cozy blankets and marshmallows for toasting. It'll be so romantic."

Trish leaned forward, her eyes sparkling with newfound inspiration. "And what about a beautiful, vintage-style reception tent? We could deck it out with fairy lights and candles, creating a warm and inviting space for the dinner and dancing. It would be like stepping into a storybook."

Nikki clasped her hands together, her heart racing with anticipation. "I love it! The tent will be perfect for keeping everyone sheltered from the cold while still maintaining that intimate atmosphere. It's exactly what I've been envisioning."

As they continued to flesh out their ideas, the three women became increasingly animated, their voices blending in a symphony of creativity and excitement. They discussed the logistics of renting the tent, the layout of the seating, and the design elements that would tie everything together. Each detail was carefully considered, from the color scheme to the table settings, as they worked to bring Nikki's vision to life.

After hours of brainstorming and planning, the trio finally sat back, their faces flushed with the thrill of their collaborative efforts.

"I can't believe how much progress we've made today," Trish remarked, a note of pride in her voice. "I think we've really nailed down the vision for the entire day."

Nikki beamed at her sister and niece. "I couldn't have done it without you two. This wedding is starting to feel like a dream come true, thanks to your help."

Amy leaned in to give Nikki a hug. "We're just getting started, Aunt Nikki. This is going to be the most beautiful and memorable wedding ever."

With the plans for the ceremony and reception taking shape, Nikki felt a renewed sense of confidence and excitement. With the unwavering support of Trish and Amy, she knew that her wedding day would be an enchanting celebration, filled with warmth, love, and the magic of winter. Nikki picked up her phone and dialed Paul's number, eagerly anticipating the chance to share the latest developments with him. After a few rings, he answered, his warm voice instantly putting a smile on her face.

"Hey, sweetheart," Paul greeted her, his voice filled with warmth. "How's wedding planning coming along?"

Nikki settled into the sofa, feeling a rush of joy as she began to recount the day's progress to him. "Paul, you won't believe how amazing everything is shaping up to be.

Trish and Amy have been incredible, and we've finalized the most magical plan for the ceremony and reception. I'm so excited!"

Paul's excitement was palpable as he responded, "That's wonderful to hear, Nikki. I can't wait to marry you and share this special day with our friends and family. It's going to be a day to remember."

Nikki's heart swelled with love at Paul's words. "I feel the same way, Paul. I'm so grateful for your support and love throughout all of this. It means the world to me."

Paul's voice softened with tenderness. "Nikki, you are my world. I can't wait to stand by your side and exchange vows with you. You're making all of my dreams come true."

As they continued to talk, their conversation was filled with sweet sentiments, laughter, and shared dreams for the future. They discussed the little details of the wedding day, each expressing their own hopes and excitement for the upcoming celebration. Nikki felt a deep sense of connection with Paul, knowing their love would be at the heart of everything on their special day.

After they said their goodbyes, Nikki sat back, her heart brimming with happiness. She was filled with a renewed sense of purpose and anticipation, knowing she and Paul were truly building a life together. As she gazed at the twinkling lights of the winter evening outside, she felt a sense of warmth and contentment she knew would only grow stronger as their wedding day drew nearer.

"Oh shoot," she shot straight up in the sofa and slapped her hand across her forehead. "I haven't told Lacy about the wedding." It had been a while since she'd spoken to Lacy so she quickly dialed Lacy's number. The phone rang a few times before Lacy's voice finally came through the line, cold and distant.

"Hey, Lacy," Nikki said, trying to steady her voice. "It's Nikki. I've been meaning to call you."

Lacy's response was guarded. "Oh, hi, Nikki."

Nikki furrowed her brows, feeling a knot forming in her stomach. "I haven't heard from you in a while. Can we meet up?"

Lacy let out a labored breath. "I don't know how possible that'll be, Nikki. I have a number of errands to run today."

"I could meet with you and help out, if you'd like," Nikki offered.

There was a brief pause on the line before Lacy asked, "What is it that you need, Nikki?" her voice curt. She felt hurt that Nikki hadn't reached out in a while.

Concern laced Nikki's voice as she took a deep breath. "Lacy, I've been so caught up with the wedding... It's only a few weeks away and there's still so much to do."

There was another brief pause on the line before Lacy's voice turned sharp. "Is that why you called, Nikki? To talk about your wedding?"

Nikki stumbled over her words, feeling her heart sink. "No, not exactly. I wanted to ask if you're okay. And to see if you'd be willing to help Trish and Amy with the wedding plans."

Lacy's response was immediate and filled with bitterness. "I'm not some charity case, Nikki. You can't just pick me up when you feel like it and then discard me when you're done."

Panicking, Nikki tried to explain herself. "Lacy, that's not what I—"

Interrupting her, Lacy's voice trembled with hurt. "As

sisters... I guess I expected too much too soon. But maybe that was my mistake. I'm not a charity case for you to feel sorry for."

Nikki felt a lump forming in her throat as Lacy's words pierced through her. The weight of her own regret intensified, and she couldn't help but recall their last meeting at the café. The rushed goodbye, the unanswered questions, and the neglected concern.

"Lacy, I'm... I'm sorry," Nikki managed to choke out, her voice thick with emotion. "I never meant to make you feel like... like a charity case."

A moment of silence hung between them before Lacy responded, her voice heavy with unshed tears. "Well, you did. I need some time, Nikki. To think, to breathe. Can we talk another time?"

"Um, sure," Nikki said. The line went dead, leaving her staring at her phone in disbelief. The lump in her throat had grown, and her heart felt heavy.

"Hey. Why do you look like your cat just died?" Amy who'd just walked into the room asked. "Wait, where's Tabby?" Her voice became panicked and her eyes wide with fear.

"Relax. Tabby's fine," Nikki breathed out. Amy had taken such a liking to Nikki's cat, sometimes it felt more like Tabby belonged to her.

"Oh, thank God" Amy breathed a sigh of relief before settling in an armchair opposite Nikki. "If it's not Tabby, what's got you looking so lost then?"

Nikki released a heavy sigh. "It's Lacy. She thinks I've been ignoring her and when I called her to invite her to be a part of the wedding, she accused me of seeing her as a charity case." Her eyes cast down to the floor as her head hung in defeat. "That was never my intent."

"Oh," Amy expressed.

"Oh?" Nikki lifted her head and raised a questioning brow.

"It's just that I kind of know that feeling, you know? Not truly knowing if your long-lost family's intentions are truly pure or just out of an act of guilt and obligation," she explained. "That's how I felt when I got here but over time and interacting with you and Mom, I realized your feelings for me are genuine. Give her time, Aunt Nikki, she'll come around."

Nikki smiled appreciatively at her niece. "Thanks, sweetie. I guess I forgot how much past hurts can affect our actions."

"Anytime young Jedi" Amy said with a glint in her eyes.

"Hey!" Nikki called out in mock offence. "If I'm a Jedi, what does that make you?"

"Emperor, of course," Amy answered automatically. "Or rather, Empress." She smiled broadly.

"All right, I'll give it to you this time...but only because you gave such good advice," Nikki conceded. But Nikki couldn't bring herself to wait on Lacy to reach out, she knew how hard that was sometimes. She had learned the hard way with Trish. The next day she found herself dialing Lacy.

After a few rings, Lacy's voice came through the line. "Hello?"

"Lacy, it's Nikki."

"Nikki," Lacy sighed.

"I know you said you needed time to think, but please just hear me out," she pleaded.

"All right," Lacy agreed.

"I've been thinking a lot about our conversation the

other day. I realized that I haven't been considerate enough of what might be going on in your life. I want to understand, and I want to be there for you. For that I am sorry."

There was a moment of silence before Lacy responded, her voice softening. "I appreciate that, Nikki. I've just been going through a lot this week, and I didn't mean to snap at you. I just didn't know how to handle everything."

"Well, I want to be there for you, if you'll let me... Trish too. We're here for you," Nikki encouraged.

"Thanks, Nikki. I'll tell you about everything soon, I promise. And about your offer to be a part of your wedding—"

"Yes?" Nikki perked up.

"I'll let you know that too," Lacy chuckled.

"All right, no rush. The spot is there for you, even if it's while I'm marching down the aisle."

"Thanks, Nikki," Lacy breathed out.

"You're welcome, Sis," Nikki smiled.

The two women hung up shortly after that, and Nikki was glad she had taken the chance to call Lacy back.

Chapter Twenty-Two

Lacy

Lacy stood in her bright, airy kitchen. The winter sunlight filtered through the sheer curtains, casting a gentle, golden glow over the room. The frigid air outside seemed to seep through the windows, a reminder of the season's chill. Mechanically, she cracked eggs into a skillet, the rhythmic sizzle providing a stark contrast to the chaotic thoughts swirling through her mind.

As she stirred the eggs, she couldn't shake the weight of guilt that hung heavily on her shoulders. She had been distant, caught up in her own emotional turmoil, and she knew she had hurt Nikki with her thoughtless words. She longed to mend the breach she had created, but every time she tried to reach out, her own tangled emotions held her back. She was happy Nikki had chosen to reach out though, and they seemed to be on the road to mending.

"David, Maria, breakfast is ready!" Lacy called out, hoping the sound of her voice would dispel the heavy silence that hung over the kitchen table. Moments later, David and Maria appeared at the table. They sat down without a word, their expressions mirroring the tension that filled the room.

Lacy placed a plate of scrambled eggs, bacon, and toast and a glass of orange juice in front of each of them, but the silence persisted as they began to eat. Lacy cast a worried glance at David, noting the stormy expression etched on his face. She knew something was wrong, but she also knew that prying would only push him further away.

After a few moments, Lacy couldn't bear the silence any longer. "David, what really happened at school?" she asked, trying to keep her tone light and non-confrontational.

David's eyes flickered up to meet hers, and she saw a flash of anger and frustration in their depths. "It's nothing, Mom. Just some stupid drama," he muttered, his tone dismissive.

Lacy sighed inwardly, but she forced herself to remain calm. "David, I'm here for you, you know that, right? If something's bothering you, you can talk to me about it."

David's jaw tightened, and for a moment, it seemed as though he might open up. But then he shook his head, pushing his plate away with a scowl. "I said it's nothing, okay? Can we just drop it?"

Lacy exchanged a worried glance with Maria, who was watching the exchange with wide eyes. She knew she couldn't push David any further without risking a blowup, but the ache of helplessness gnawed at her insides.

As they finished their breakfast in strained silence, Lacy's thoughts churned with the weight of her own struggles. David's troubles at school, the uncertain future of his swimming career, and her own tangled emotions about Phillip all loomed over her like a storm cloud, threatening to engulf her.

As she cleared the breakfast dishes, the weight of uncertainty pressed down on her shoulders, and she wondered how she could possibly navigate the storm that raged within and around her.

After dropping Maria off at elementary school, Lacy took a deep breath and steered her car toward Camano High. The drive was a blur of worry and apprehension, her mind consumed by the impending meeting with the school authorities. As she parked in the bustling lot, she felt a surge of anxiety knotting her stomach.

Stepping out of the car, Lacy smoothed down her skirt and squared her shoulders, steeling herself for the difficult conversation ahead. She made her way through the grand set of double doors and into the main office, where the secretary greeted her with a sympathetic smile.

"Good morning, Mrs. Lopez," the secretary said as she rose from her desk. "Principal Johnson and Coach Samson are waiting for you in the principal's office. I'll take you there."

Lacy nodded her thanks, her nerves tightening with each step that brought her closer to the meeting. When they arrived at the principal's office, she was ushered inside and greeted by the stern, no-nonsense figure of Principal Johnson and the rugged, earnest face of Coach Samson.

"Good morning, Mrs. Lopez," Principal Johnson said with a slight nod. "Please, have a seat. We need to discuss the incident involving your son, David."

Lacy took a seat, her stomach churning with apprehension. She braced herself for the stern reprimand she expected to receive.

"Mrs. Lopez, I want to make it clear that we do not condone violence of any form at Camano High," Principal Johnson began, his voice firm but not unkind. "However, Coach Samson has shed some light on the circumstances surrounding the altercation, and I understand there were extenuating circumstances."

Coach Samson leaned forward, his expression grave. "Mrs. Lopez, the student David punched made a remark about him not being a good swimmer and implied I took pity on him because of his father's passing," he explained, his voice tinged with frustration. "I want to assure you that I would never show favoritism based on sympathy. David is a talented swimmer in his own right. He's only been on the team for a few weeks, and I can definitely understand why. He is such a talented swimmer. His dedication is what I value."

Lacy's heart clenched at the revelation, a surge of anger and protectiveness rising within her. "I can't believe someone would stoop so low as to use my son's tragedy against him," she murmured, her voice thick with emotion.

Principal Johnson nodded in agreement. "It's a despicable tactic, and I assure you, it will not go unpunished. However, given the circumstances, we have decided on a more lenient punishment for David. He will be placed in in-house suspension, so he will remain at school under supervision. We haven't decided if he'll be let back on the team for this term though."

Lacy breathed a sigh of relief; grateful the consequences weren't more severe. "Thank you, Principal Johnson, Coach Samson," she said earnestly. "I appreciate your understanding and your efforts to handle this situation fairly."

As she left the office, a mixture of emotions churned within her—relief David's punishment wasn't more severe, anger at the callousness of the other student, and a deep-seated determination to support her son through whatever challenges lay ahead. She knew they had weathered storms before, and they would weather this one too.

Lacy's heart was still heavy with worry and frustration as she pulled into the driveway. As she stepped out of the car, her eyes landed on a familiar figure standing on her front porch. Phillip, with his warm brown eyes and reassuring smile, was waiting for her. The sight of him sent a wave of relief through her, and she quickened her pace to reach him.

"Phillip," she murmured as she approached, her voice catching with emotion. Without a word, she stepped into his open arms, seeking the comfort and strength that his presence always seemed to offer.

"Lacy, what's wrong?" Phillip asked, his voice gentle as he held her close. "You look like you've been through a lot."

Lacy took a deep breath, her words tumbling out in a rush as she recounted the meeting at David's school and the hurtful incident that had led to his outburst. "I just can't believe someone would use David's loss against him like that," she said, her voice thick with emotion. "It's been so hard for him, and now this..."

Phillip's embrace tightened around her, offering silent support as he spoke. "Lacy, I know this is tough, but David needs you to be strong for him," he said softly. "He's going through a lot, but he also needs to figure out how to deal with the hurt and anger in a way that won't hurt him further or get him in trouble."

Lacy nodded against his chest. "I know you're right. I just don't know how to reach him. We were making such good progress and then this happened, and it feels like we might just be back at square one," she confessed.

"You can't let this break you apart. You've both been through so much, but I can assure you that David needs you—a lot, even if he doesn't show it," Phillip spoke encouragingly.

"Thanks, Phillip," she breathed out.

"Anytime," he responded.

As she pulled back slightly, she found herself gazing into Phillip's eyes, the warmth and understanding in his gaze drawing her in. In that moment, the air between them crackled with unspoken emotion, and Lacy felt a rush of something stirring within her.

Their faces drew closer, their breaths mingling in the space between them. It felt like the most natural thing in the world, a moment suspended in time, until a voice shattered the fragile bubble they had created.

"Mom?" David's voice called out from behind them, and Lacy jumped back, her cheeks flushing with embarrassment.

David stood at the front door; his expression unreadable. "What's going on?"

Lacy straightened, trying to compose herself as she turned toward her son. "David. We were just... talking," she said, her voice unsteady. "Why are you home?"

David's gaze shifted between his mother and Phillip, a mix of curiosity and suspicion in his eyes. "Talking about what?" he asked, his tone edged with a hint of skepticism. Lacy exchanged a quick glance with Phillip, her mind racing to find the right words.

"We were discussing what happened at school today, David." David's jaw clenched, and he cast a wary look at Phillip.

"I'm sorry about what happened to you, David. I know we're not that close, but if you ever need someone to talk to, to get a male's perspective on things, I want you to know that I'm here for you," Phillip offered.

David's gaze remained fixed on Phillip for a moment longer before he sighed and looked away. "Whatever. It's not a big deal."

Lacy took a step toward her son, concern etched on her face. "David, it is a big deal. You're my son, and I want to make sure you're okay. If there's anything you need to talk about, or if you're feeling overwhelmed, I'm here for you."

David shrugged; a defensive barrier evident in his posture. "I don't need a therapy session. Can we just drop it?" Lacy sighed, recognizing the familiar pattern of her son closing himself off.

"Okay, I won't push. But just remember, I'm here for you whenever you're ready to talk." As David headed for the kitchen, Lacy turned back to Phillip, gratitude in her eyes. "Thank you for being here, Phillip. I don't know what I would do without your support."

Phillip smiled reassuringly. "Lacy, I care about you and your family. I want you to understand that."

Lacy gave him a grateful smile.

After Phillip left, Lacy turned to find David standing

in the doorway, his expression a mix of concern and curiosity. She braced herself for the questions she knew were coming, but to her surprise, David simply stepped forward and enveloped her in a tight embrace.

"Mom, I know it's not what it looks like," David said quietly, his voice muffled against her shoulder. "I just wanted to say thank you for always being in my corner, even though I've been acting like a jerk lately."

Lacy returned the hug, feeling a surge of love and protectiveness toward her son. "David, you don't have to thank me for that. I'll always be here for you, no matter what," she murmured, her voice filled with emotion.

"It's just that guy, what he said, it really got under my skin and I just lost it. It won't happen again. I promise," he spoke, the hurt and anger in his tone tearing Lacy's heart.

"I know, honey. I'm sorry you had to go through that, but I'm glad you're okay."

As they pulled back, David met her gaze, his eyes searching hers. "Mom, I gotta be honest. The idea of you dating, being with anyone other than Dad... it's strange to me," he admitted, his voice tinged with vulnerability. "But I'll support you, I promise."

Lacy reached out to cup his cheek, her heart swelling with love for her son. "David, I'm not trying to replace your dad. No one could ever take his place in our hearts," she said gently.

David nodded, a small, understanding smile tugging at his lips. "I know, Mom. I know."

In that moment, a sense of closeness and understanding enveloped them, a silent reassurance that they would weather whatever challenges lay ahead, together.

As they lingered in the embrace, a tentative smile broke across David's face. "Oh, Mom, I almost forgot to tell you. Coach decided to let me back on the swim team. He said he believes in me and I deserve a second chance."

Lacy's eyes lit up with pride and relief. "David, that's wonderful news! I'm so proud of you," she exclaimed, pulling him into another hug. "You've worked so hard for this, and I know you'll make the most of this opportunity."

As they released each other, a sense of hope and renewed strength filled the air. Lacy knew, despite the challenges they faced, they would find their way through, buoyed by the love and support that bound them together.

Chapter Twenty-Three

Lacy

L acy's heart pounded as she approached Nikki's front door. She took a deep breath and rang the doorbell, her mind racing with a million thoughts. When Nikki opened the door, the sisters shared a long, meaningful embrace.

"Lacy, it's so good to see you," Nikki said, her eyes filled with warmth and concern.

"I've missed you so much," Lacy replied, her voice barely above a whisper.

Nikki ushered her inside, where Trish and Amy were gathered in the living room.

"Lacy, David, Maria. What a lovely surprise," Trish gave out as she jumped up to hug each of them. Amy did the same.

"Hey, Aunt Trish, Amy." David, gave one of his infectious smiles causing Lacy's heart to flutter with gratitude.

"Hi, sweetie," Trish said, ruffling his hair. "And, Maria, look how much you've grown!" Maria beamed. Trish turned to Lacy then. "Welcome back, Lacy," Trish said, her voice tinged with relief. "We've missed you."

Lacy's eyes filled with tears as she looked at her sisters and her niece. "I'm so sorry for everything," she said, her voice catching in her throat.

Nikki reached out and squeezed Lacy's hand. "It's okay, Lacy. We understand. Life can be tough, and we know you've been through a lot. We're also sorry for not being more sensitive to your situation."

Trish nodded in agreement. "We're just glad you're here now. That's what matters."

Lacy felt a weight lift off her shoulders as she gazed at her supportive sisters. "Thank you, both of you. I don't know what I'd do without you."

The sisters spent the rest of the evening catching up, sharing stories, and making plans for the wedding. As they laughed and reminisced, Lacy felt a renewed sense of hope and belonging. She knew that with her sisters by her side, anything was possible.

As the evening sun cast its glow through the windows, the sisters gathered in the living room, the air buzzing with excitement and anticipation. Lacy's heart swelled with gratitude for the warmth and understanding she had received from her sisters. She took a deep breath and turned to Nikki with a grateful smile.

"Thank you, Nikki. I'm really grateful for the opportunity to help with the wedding," Lacy said, her eyes shimmering with appreciation.

Nikki hugged her tightly. "I'm just happy to know you're willing to be a part of this, Lacy. Your expertise will be invaluable. If I had known sooner that you were an event planner, you would have been in charge of my wedding from the start."

Lacy returned the hug, feeling a surge of warmth. "I'm eager to contribute, Nikki. I want to make this day as special as possible for you."

Nikki beamed.

Lacy's eyes sparkled with curiosity. "So, tell me, what's been planned so far? The wedding is only a few weeks away, and we don't have much time to get everything together."

Nikki nodded, her enthusiasm bubbling over. "Well, I've been thinking a lot about the theme. I really want a vintage vibe for the wedding. I've been collecting antique decorations and envisioning a romantic, timeless atmosphere."

Trish chimed in, her eyes lighting up. "The venue we chose is the lawn and garden at the back of the inn. It has a beautiful rustic charm that will complement the vintage theme perfectly."

Lacy's mind began to whirl with ideas. "That sounds wonderful, Nikki. Vintage is such a classic and elegant choice. I can already picture the lace, the old-fashioned flowers, and the soft, muted color palette."

Nikki nodded eagerly. "Exactly! I've been collecting vintage lace doilies, old-fashioned teacups, and antique frames for the table centerpieces. I want everything to feel like it's been plucked from a bygone era."

Lacy's eyes gleamed with excitement. "I love that idea. It's going to create such a romantic and nostalgic atmosphere. And those elements will make for stunning photographs as well."

Nikki's face lit up with joy. "I'm so glad you think so.

I've been pouring my heart into these plans, and I can't wait to see it all come together."

The sisters spent the rest of the evening poring over the details of the vintage theme, exchanging ideas and inspirations. Lacy's mind brimmed with creativity as she envisioned the magical ambiance they could create.

As the evening unfolded, Lacy watched with a warm heart as her family gathered in the living room, filling the space with laughter and joyful chatter. David and Amy had found common ground in their shared experience of discovering their extended family. They sat together on the sofa, engrossed in conversation.

"I still can't believe we just found out about each other," Amy said, her eyes shining with excitement. "It's so amazing to have a new cousin like you, David."

David grinned. "Yeah, it's pretty wild. I never thought I'd have family I didn't even know about."

"Well, I never thought I would find a family that actually loved me and wanted me around. My adoptive parents weren't so great," she expressed, an uncharacteristic sadness passing over her face. "But that's that. I've never been this happy and that's what matters now."

"It sure is." Trish walked over to place a loving kiss against her daughter's forehead. Amy smiled appreciatively.

"That's a really cool story." David grinned.

"Right?" Amy laughed.

Lacy watched them with a smile, grateful for the bond that was forming between her son and her niece. It was a beautiful reminder of the power of the importance of family. She had lost two important pieces of her family, but here she was gaining more than she had bargained for.

Meanwhile, Maria sat nearby, her eyes wide with

admiration as she listened to Amy speak. After a moment, Maria gathered the courage to join the conversation.

"So, you're studying to be a pastry chef? That's so cool," Maria said, her voice filled with awe.

Amy beamed at Maria's enthusiasm. "Thanks, Maria! I love baking, and I'm learning all about making delicious pastries and desserts. If you ever want to learn some baking tips, I'd be happy to show you."

Maria's face lit up with excitement. "I'd love that! I'm really into baking too, and art—mostly art—but I want to learn more about baking too. Maybe you can teach me your secret recipes!"

As Amy and Maria bonded over their shared passion for baking, Lacy felt a swell of happiness in her chest. It was heartwarming to see her children connecting with their newfound cousin and forming meaningful relationships.

Amidst the lively conversations, Nikki turned to Lacy with a radiant smile. "Lacy, I've been meaning to ask you. Would you do me the honor of being one of my bridesmaids?"

Lacy's eyes widened in surprise, her heart fluttering with joy. "Nikki, are you sure?"

"Of course, I'm sure," Nikki spoke confidently.

"Then I would be absolutely thrilled to be one of your bridesmaids," Lacy beamed.

Nikki enveloped Lacy in a warm embrace, her eyes filled with gratitude. "Thank you, Lacy. Having you there means the world to me."

As the evening melted into night, the family continued to share stories, laughter, and dreams for the upcoming wedding. Lacy felt a renewed sense of belonging and purpose, knowing she would be standing beside her sister on her big day, surrounded by the love and support of her cherished family.

As the conversations continued to flow, Lacy found herself engaged in a heart-to-heart with Trish. They reminisced about their childhood, sharing stories of the adventures they'd had growing up in different states.

Trish's gaze shifted to the group of youngsters chatting animatedly. "I'm so glad the kids are getting along. It's heartwarming to see them bonding over their shared experiences. It's like they've known each other for years."

Lacy's eyes followed Trish's gaze, landing on David, Amy, and Maria. The sight filled her with an indescribable sense of joy and contentment. She was grateful her children were finding their place within this extended family, and she knew the new connections would enrich their lives in ways she couldn't yet imagine.

Lacy returned home from her visit with her sisters, her mind still filled with the warmth of their embrace and the joy of reconnecting. She settled into her cozy living room, the memories of the evening swirling in her mind. After a moment's hesitation, she picked up her phone and dialed Phillip's number.

The phone rang a few times before Phillip answered. "Hey, Lacy. How'd it go?" he asked.

"It went really well, Phillip," Lacy replied, her voice suffused with a mixture of contentment and uncertainty. "I'm going to be very involved in the wedding. I'll be walking down the aisle with a groomsman, but he's married. So, I was wondering if you'd like to be my plus one."

There was a brief pause on the other end of the line before Phillip spoke. "Lacy, what does that mean for us?"

Lacy hesitated, choosing her words carefully. "It's not a date, Phillip. We would be going as friends."

Phillip took a moment before responding. "I appreciate the invitation, Lacy, but I think it's best if I decline. I don't want there to be any confusion about what we are, and I believe accepting would be treading dangerous waters."

Lacy's heart sank, but she understood where he was coming from. "I understand, Phillip. I don't want things to be complicated either."

There was a moment of silence before Phillip spoke again. "I hope you have a great time at the wedding, Lacy. And if you need anything, I'm here for you."

"Thank you, Phillip. I appreciate that," Lacy replied, her voice soft with gratitude.

After saying their goodbyes, Lacy set her phone down with a sigh. She knew Phillip was right, but it didn't make the disappointment any easier to bear. She had hoped they could attend the wedding together, but she respected his decision.

The following afternoon, Lacy was surprised by a knock on her front door. When she opened it, she found Phillip standing there with a hopeful smile.

"Hey, Lacy," he greeted. "I was thinking, despite the cold, it might be nice if we went for a walk by the beach. What do you say?"

Lacy's eyes widened in surprise. She hadn't expected Phillip to visit her so soon after their conversation. She glanced over at David, who was sitting on the couch, engrossed in a book.

David looked up and met Lacy's gaze. "Go on, Mom. Have some fun. I'll be fine here."

Lacy smiled gratefully at her son. "Thank you, David. I won't be long."

As they strolled along the beach, the cold air nipped at their faces, and they wrapped their coats tightly around themselves, seeking warmth.

"I really enjoy spending time with you, Lacy," Phillip said, breaking the silence between them. "I've been thinking a lot about our conversation yesterday. Would it be too forward of me to say that I'm developing feelings for you?"

Lacy's heart skipped a beat at Phillip's words. She had been hesitant to fully admit her own feelings, fearing things might move too fast. But now, with the cold wind whipping around them, she felt a surge of courage.

"No, Phillip, it's not too forward," Lacy replied, her voice soft and sincere. "I'm developing feelings for you too."

Phillip's face lit up with joy, and he took hold of Lacy's hand. They continued walking along the icy shore, the rhythm of their footsteps matching the growing excitement within their hearts.

As they reached a more secluded spot, surrounded by the quiet beauty of the beach, Phillip came to a stop. His eyes met Lacy's, searching for confirmation.

"Lacy, if I accept your plus one invitation, does that mean it's a date?" he asked, his voice full of hope and anticipation.

Lacy laughed in response to Phillip's question, her voice carrying through the chilly air. "Yes, Phillip. It means it's a date. With you."

Phillip's grin widened, unable to contain his happiness. He gently brushed a strand of hair behind Lacy's ear before leaning in slowly, allowing their lips to meet in a soft, lingering kiss. The world around them seemed to fade away as they lost themselves in that moment.

When they finally pulled apart, their faces flushed and their smiles radiant, Lacy felt a warmth spreading through her veins. She looked into Phillip's eyes, feeling a growing sense of connection and possibility.

"Phillip, I'm really happy. I want to see where this takes us," Lacy said, her voice filled with a mix of excitement and vulnerability. "But let's take it slow, okay?"

Phillip nodded, his gaze unwavering. "Absolutely, Lacy. I'm completely on board with that."

As they resumed their walk, hand in hand, the cold air surrounding them seemed to carry an underlying promise of warmth and adventure. Lacy couldn't help but feel a sense of wonder at the unfolding of their newfound relationship.

Chapter Twenty-Four

Nikki

"Nikki, you look absolutely breathtaking! Paul won't be able to take his eyes off you," Trish complimented her sister as she stared at her through the floor-to-ceiling closet mirror, a warm smile gracing her face.

"You think so?" Nikki asked. Staring at herself in the mirror. She had chosen a beautiful, blue chiffon dress that cupped her upper torso before flaring at the waist and stopping at her calf and three-inch strappy gold heels.

"Are you kidding me?" Trish raised a brow as she stared back at her. "Paul won't be able to take his eyes off you this evening."

"Thanks, Trish." Nikki smiled appreciatively.

"Let me help you with that." Trish held out her hand for the jewelry box and Nikki gave it to her. She held out her wrist so Trish could snap on the gold bracelet Paul had gotten her. "Trust me, Paul is going to be blown away by you."

"Well, not too far, I hope. I still need him to be present for this date," Nikki joked and Trish joined in.

After helping her to apply some light makeup, Trish stepped back to admire her work. "You are absolutely stunning," she reiterated. Nikki smiled broadly. Just then the doorbell rang.

"That must be him," Nikki breathed out, her heart racing with excitement.

"I'll get it. You take your time and make a grand entrance," Trish instructed.

Nikki stared at herself in the mirror once more, ensuring she liked what she saw before heading for the foyer. She found Paul standing there, looking quite handsome in a crisp white shirt and tailored trousers. His eyes lit up as he took in her appearance.

"Wow, Nikki, you look absolutely stunning," Paul breathed, his voice filled with admiration and affection.

Nikki blushed as her heart fluttered at his words. "Thank you, Paul. You look very handsome." It was his turn to blush.

"These are for you," he said, handing her a bouquet of roses.

Nikki accepted the roses with a grateful smile. The vibrant colors and sweet fragrance enveloped her senses, heightening her anticipation for their upcoming evening together. Unable to resist the pull of their connection, she closed the distance between them, capturing Paul's lips in a gentle kiss.

As they pulled away, their love still evident in their

lingering gaze, Nikki couldn't help but quell her curiosity. "So, where are you taking me tonight?" she inquired, her voice filled with excitement.

An impish grin played on Paul's lips as he replied, "It's a surprise, my love. Trust me, you'll never forget this night."

Nikki nodded, smiling warmly at him. "I trust you completely, Paul. But can I have a little hint, just to satisfy my curiosity?"

Paul chuckled, his eyes dancing mischievously. "Patience, my love. You'll get your hint soon enough," he teased, enjoying the playful banter between them.

"I'll put these in water for you," Trish, who had been standing by, said, taking the roses from Nikki. "You two have fun." She smiled encouragingly.

Paul led her outside and courteously held the car door open for her. Nikki gracefully stepped into the luxurious SUV. She settled into the plush seats, her excitement soaring as they pulled away from the serene beauty of Camano Island and onto the bustling highway leading to Seattle.

Curiosity took hold of her again, and Nikki turned to Paul, her eyes sparkling with intrigue. "Paul, are we heading to Seattle?"

Paul grinned; his eyes filled with anticipation. "Buckle up, Nikki. It's going to be a night filled with surprises and memories," he replied cryptically.

Nikki settled back into her seat, her mind buzzing with excitement. She trusted Paul completely, knowing that whatever he had in store for her would be magical. Their conversation flowed effortlessly, a mixture of laughter, dreams, and shared gestures of love. Each passing mile brought them closer to a night that would create cherished memories, deepening their bond as they celebrated their love amidst the vibrant city lights of Seattle.

As they arrived in Seattle, the city's familiar skyline came into view, its skyscrapers illuminated against the night sky. Nikki appreciated the urban beauty as they traversed the bustling streets.

"Seattle at night is always so captivating," Nikki remarked, her eyes taking in the familiar sights with a sense of appreciation.

Paul nodded, a glint of excitement in his eyes. "Absolutely, but just wait until you see what I have planned for tonight."

As they approached their destination, Nikki's gaze was drawn to the twinkling lights across the water, creating a shimmering reflection. "The waterfront looks so stunning at night," she observed, her voice filled with admiration.

Paul smiled, nodding in agreement. "It's a beautiful sight, isn't it? But I think our evening is about to get even better."

Their journey led them to the iconic Space Needle, a structure Nikki had visited before, but never at night. "We're heading to the restaurant up there, aren't we?" she asked, her eyes alight with anticipation.

Paul nodded, pleased she had guessed his plan. "You got it. I thought it would be a special spot for us tonight."

Nikki appreciated Paul's thoughtful choice of venue. "Paul, this is wonderful. I've always wanted to see the city from up there at night. Thank you for making tonight so memorable," she expressed, feeling grateful for the effort he had put into their evening.

Together, they entered the Space Needle, the anticipation thick in the air. As they ascended the floors, the muffled sounds of conversation and the soft music playing in the background serenaded their journey. The glass walls of the elevator revealed glimpses of the cityscape, each floor bringing them closer to their dining experience. Nikki held tightly to Paul's hand, her excitement growing with each passing second.

As the elevator doors opened on the top floor, Nikki's eyes widened in awe. The panoramic view of the city unfolded before her, the twinkling lights stretching as far as the eye could see. The restaurant, with its elegant ambiance and warm lighting, felt like an intimate sanctuary amidst the vastness of the city.

Paul led her to their table, his eyes never leaving Nikki's, their connection deepening with every step. "Here we are, my love," he murmured, pulling out her chair like a true gentleman.

Nikki took her seat, her gaze shifting from the cityscape to Paul. "Paul, it's beyond anything I could have imagined. Thank you for making this night so special," she expressed, her voice filled with genuine gratitude.

He reached across the table, gently grasping her hand. "It's my pleasure, Nikki. Tonight is about celebrating our love and creating memories that will last a lifetime," he replied, his voice filled with tenderness.

As they settled into their evening, surrounded by the breathtaking views and the warmth of their love, Nikki couldn't help but feel an overwhelming sense of enchantment. This night, this moment, was a testament to the beautiful chapter they were about to embark on together —a chapter where their love would continue to grow amidst the splendor of everyday life.

A friendly server approached their table, a warm

smile gracing her face. "Good evening, and welcome to Space Needle. My name is Emily, and I'll be your server tonight. May I start you off with some drinks?" she asked, her voice filled with cheery anticipation.

Paul glanced at Nikki, a loving sparkle in his eyes. "We will begin with a glass of champagne," he ordered, his voice exuding delight.

Nikki nodded, her excitement palpable. "That sounds wonderful, Paul," she replied, her eyes never leaving his. "I can't think of a better way to celebrate this special night."

He selected the most suitable one from the drink menu and their server left to get it. She returned with their drinks, expertly pouring the sparkling liquid into their flutes. As they clinked their glasses together, a symphony of fizzing bubbles filled the air, symbolizing their love and shared excitement.

The menus were presented, and Paul took the lead, recommending some of the chef's specialties. Their server, Emily, expertly guided them through the exquisite choices, her knowledge of the menu enhancing their anticipation.

"This seared scallop dish is absolutely divine," Paul exclaimed, a twinkle of delight in his eyes. "The delicate sweetness of the scallops is perfectly complemented by the richness of the sauce. You have to try this, Nikki."

Nikki smiled, her eyes sparkling as she watched her chef fiancé turn their dinner into an epicurean delight.

Throughout the evening, their server, Emily, attended to their needs with grace and professionalism, ensuring their culinary journey was seamless. As the courses changed, the conversations flowed effortlessly, filled with laughter and genuine appreciation for the culinary artistry before them.

As they savored their final moments of the night, their hearts and bellies full, Nikki couldn't help but feel a deep sense of gratitude for the incredible experience they had shared. The evening had surpassed their wildest expectations, leaving them with memories they would cherish for a lifetime.

Nikki looked into Paul's eyes, her fingers tracing circles on her wine glass. "You know, Paul, I thought I had found love once before," she began, her voice soft.

Paul's gaze was filled with understanding, his hand reaching across the table to hold hers.

Nikki took a deep breath, her eyes searching his. "When I married my first husband, I thought it was because I was in love. But looking back now, I realize I was searching for someone who was the opposite of my father, someone he would despise. It was all a façade," she admitted, her voice tinged with remorse.

Paul's touch grew tighter, his eyes filled with empathy. "Nikki, I can't imagine how hard it must have been for you to let go of that relationship. But I'm grateful you found the strength to acknowledge your true feelings," he said sincerely.

A small smile graced Nikki's lips. "It took a lot of time and tears, finding out about my condition and him having an affair, but I finally admitted the truth to myself," she confessed. "I vowed never to get involved with anyone again. And then, you entered my life again, Paul."

Paul's voice was tender, his eyes reflecting the depth of his emotions. "Nikki, after Sarah's mother passed away, I thought I had lost my chance at love. She was everything to me, and her absence left an indescribable void in my heart. And then you came back."

Nikki's hand instinctively caressed Paul's hand lying on the table.

Paul's gaze met hers, his voice steady with conviction. "Nikki, I never want to let you go. You are my present and my future. I can't wait for you to be Mrs. Thompson," he declared, his voice filled with unwavering love.

A radiant smile lit up Nikki's face as she held Paul's gaze. "I can't wait either, Paul. To commit my life to you, to share every joy and challenge that comes our way," she responded, her voice laced with excitement.

Their hands remained intertwined as they sat there, immersed in the afterglow of their heartfelt conversation. The world seemed to fade away, leaving only the two of them in their own love-filled bubble.

Soft music saturated the room, further adding to the romantic ambiance. Paul's eyes sparkled with affection as he reached out his hand toward Nikki. "May I have this dance?" he asked, a playful smile dancing on his lips.

Nikki's heart skipped a beat, her own smile matching his. "I would love to," she replied, her voice filled with anticipation and excitement.

The soft melody of a jazzy love song enveloped them as they moved gracefully on the dance floor. In Paul's arms, Nikki felt like the luckiest woman in the world. The iconic voice of Frank Sinatra singing "I've Got You Under My Skin" filled the air, affirming the depth of their love.

As they swayed together, their bodies perfectly in sync, the outside world melted away, leaving only the two of them in their own enchanting bubble of love. With each step, their connection deepened, their hearts dancing to the rhythm of their unwavering affection.

Paul's gaze never wavered from Nikki's, his voice a

warm whisper. "Are you having a good time, my love?" he asked, his eyes filled with adoration.

Nikki's smile widened, her heart overflowing with joy. "The best time, Paul. Tonight has been a dream come true," she replied, her voice laced with genuine emotion.

Chapter Twenty-Five

Nikki

Nikki, Trish, and Lacy stood together in the peaceful serenity of the Camano Lutheran cemetery. They felt the soft whisper of the wind rustling through the trees, carrying with it a sense of solace and reminiscence. They gazed at the headstones that marked the final resting place of their parents, feeling a mix of emotions stirring within them.

With a gentle smile, Nikki broke the silence, her eyes fixated on her father's grave. "Oh, Dad, how many times I've wished you were here so you could see all the things I've accomplished," she began, her voice filled with determination. "You always doubted my dreams of becoming a good journalist, but here I stand, living proof that I made it. I was even editor-in-chief for a brief stint," she chuckled. "The funny thing is, I gave it all up because I realized family is more important to me than any job or reputation. Because without family you are nothing."

Trish nodded, her gaze flickering between her sister and her parents' graves. Tears welled up in her eyes as she mustered the strength to speak her truth. "I've carried this burden for so long, Mom and Dad," she said, her voice quivering. "You made me give up my baby, my own flesh and blood. I was only nineteen, forced to be an adult, when all I needed was your love and support. How could you abandon me like that?"

Nikki rushed over to hug Trish as tears that welled up in her eyes began to fall.

Lacy looked at her newfound sisters, her heart heavy with the gravity of their shared pain. Taking a deep breath, she stepped closer to the gravesite of their parents, her voice laced with both sadness and gratitude. "I never knew you, Dad," she admitted, her voice trembling. "But somehow, through the cracks of your mistakes, you brought my sisters into my life. I see how fiercely they love, how loyal they are to one another, and I'm grateful I have them in my life. Thank you for that."

As their words hung in the air, a poignant silence enveloped them. The weight of their shared experiences, their longing for the love they never received echoed through the cemetery. Yet, amidst the sorrow, there was also a glimmer of hope, a sense of closure gradually settling upon their hearts.

Nikki turned to Trish, her eyes filled with pride and love. "Trish, you did what you had to do. You've carried that pain on your shoulders for far too long," she said, her voice filled with empathy. "But today, here in this sacred place, we can let it go and heal together. We have each other now, and that, my sisters, is something truly beautiful."

A tear trickled down Trish's cheek as she reached out to squeeze Nikki's hand tightly. "You're right," she whispered, her voice choked with emotion. "We've come so far, and I am so grateful to have you by my side, Nikki, and you, Lacy," she turned to look at her.

Lacy, who had been silently observing the profound bond between her newfound sisters, felt a warmth blossoming within her. Stepping forward, she wrapped her arms around both Nikki and Trish, holding them in a heartfelt embrace. "We may have suffered, but look at how far we've come," she murmured, her voice filled with awe. "We are strong, resilient, and we have each other. Together, we can face anything."

"I believe that with all my heart," Nikki affirmed.

Leaving the cemetery behind, the trio locked eyes, sharing a moment of unspoken understanding. Their journey had just begun, but their hearts were now lighter, having poured out their long-held pains at their parents' graves.

"I have an idea of what could take our minds off this painful but liberating experience," Trish suggested.

"What do you have in mind?" Nikki asked.

"Let's go to Kristofferson Farm."

"Okay. I'm game," Nikki accepted.

"Me too," Lacy joined.

As the sisters got into Nikki's car, they made their way toward the Kristofferson Farm, a sense of anticipation filled the air. The gravel crunching beneath the wheels through the quiet countryside matched the rhythm of their beating hearts. The landscape before them was a tapestry of golden hues as the midday sun cast its warm glow upon the rolling fields and the iconic red barn that stood proudly against the horizon.

Nikki paused for a moment, taking in the familiar sight before them. "It feels like a lifetime ago," she remarked, her voice tinged with nostalgia. "This place holds so many memories."

Trish nodded, a small smile playing on her lips. "Remember all the adventures we had here when we were younger?" she asked, her eyes sparkling. "Running through the fields, climbing trees, and chasing fireflies at night?"

"Yeah. I do. Dad had been more loving and lenient then," Nikki surmised with a bittersweet smile.

Lacy chimed in; her voice filled with excitement. "I can't wait to experience it all with you, to make new memories together."

The chilly winds of February swept across Camano Island as Nikki, Lacy, and Trish made their way to the picturesque Kristofferson Farm. The air held a lingering crispness from the winter season, but signs of spring were beginning to emerge. Most of the ice had melted, leaving behind patches of green grass and the promise of new beginnings.

As the sisters pulled into the gravel driveway of the farm, they were met with the sight of sprawling fields and charming barns. The farm was famous for its seasonal activities, and even in the early days of February, there were plenty of things to do.

Nikki led the way, her excitement palpable. "I've heard so much about Kristofferson Farm. They offer all sorts of activities for families. We can take a ride to see the animals, wander through the bakery, and even try our hand at making some pies or baking bread."

Lacy's eyes widened at the thought of all the fun to be had. "I can't wait to go to the bakery and see the all fresh pastries, breads, and pies. It'll be a great way to spend the weekend together."

Trish nodded, her smile mirroring their enthusiasm. "I've always wanted to revisit the farm. This is the perfect opportunity to reconnect and make new memories."

As they approached the entrance, a friendly staff member greeted them with a warm smile. "Welcome to Kristofferson Farm! My name is Sarah. How can I help you today?"

Nikki returned the smile, her eyes shining with excitement. "We're here for a day of fun! We heard about the animals, the bakery, and pastry making. Can you tell us more about what's available?"

Sarah's face lit up as she eagerly shared the details. "Absolutely! We have hayrides that take you on a scenic tour of the farm, giving you a chance to see the beautiful countryside. You can visit the animals and feed them if you like. And over at the bakery, we're offering hot chocolate with fresh pastries. You can also learn how to make fresh bread or make an apple pie from the farm's delicious apples."

The sisters exchanged excited glances, their anticipation growing. "That all sounds wonderful," Lacy chimed in. "We'd love to do it all, if possible."

Sarah grinned. "That's fantastic! You're in for a day full of fun and adventure. The hayrides run every hour, so you won't have to wait long. As for the cider pressing, you can join in at any time and learn the process from our experienced staff."

Nikki clapped her hands in delight. "Wonderful!

We'll start with the hayride. And cider pressing can be the grand finale."

As they made their way to the starting point of the hayride, the sisters couldn't help but share their excitement and make plans for the day. They talked and laughed; their voices filled with anticipation.

Once on the hayride, they marveled at the stunning views of the farm. Rolling fields, and vibrant flowers. The gentle rhythm of the horse's hooves and the fresh country air made them feel alive and connected to the earth.

At the pumpkin patch, the sisters wandered through rows of plump, orange pumpkins, carefully selecting their favorites. Laughter filled the air as they compared pumpkins and playfully teased each other about their choices.

Finally, they made their way to the barn for the bread making demonstration. The scent of apples filled the air, mingling with the cozy warmth of the barn. With eager smiles, they listened attentively as the staff explained the pie process, from preparing the apples to mixing the crust and assembling the pies.

As the day drew to a close, the sisters gathered their pies and shared their gratitude for the wonderful experiences they had enjoyed. The farm had provided the perfect backdrop for reconnecting and making new memories, strengthening the bond between the three sisters.

As they made their way back to the car, the sun set over the horizon, casting a golden glow over the farmlands. Nikki turned to her sisters, a contented smile on her face. "I'm grateful for moments like these, when we can come together and create new memories. Today was a day to remember."

Trish and Lacy nodded in agreement, their hearts

full. "Absolutely," Trish said with a smile. "No matter what the future holds, we'll always have these moments of joy and togetherness."

With a final glimpse at the farm, the siblings climbed into the car, their hearts lighter and their spirits lifted. As they drove away from Kristofferson Farm, the bond between the sisters grew stronger, nourished by the experiences they had shared on that beautiful Camano Island day.

After bidding farewell to Lacy and dropping her off at Livingston Bay Shore Drive, Nikki and Trish continued their journey home, the memories of the day at Kristofferson Farm still fresh in their minds.

The car ride was filled with a comfortable silence as they reflected on the day's events. The sun began to set, casting a warm, golden glow over the countryside. The beauty of the moment seemed to amplify the depth of their shared experiences, making their bond as sisters feel even stronger.

As they pulled into the driveway of Trish's home, Amy, Trish's daughter, eagerly rushed out to greet them. She had been eagerly waiting to hear all about their outing and bonding time with Lacy.

Amy's eyes sparkled with excitement as she exclaimed, "How was your day? Did you have a great time at the farm?"

Nikki smiled warmly at her niece; her heart touched by her enthusiasm. "Oh, Amy, it was absolutely wonderful. We had the best time at Kristofferson Farm. We went on an incredible hayride, visited the animals, watched a bread making demonstration, and even made apple pies. It was a day filled with laughter, joy, and special moments."

Amy's face lit up as she listened to Nikki's animated retelling of their adventures. "I wish I could have come with you. It sounds like so much fun!"

Trish joined the conversation, her eyes filled with affection for her daughter. "We missed you too, sweetie. But don't worry, we will plan more outings like this in the future. We want to make sure we include you and create new memories together."

Amy nodded eagerly, her excitement building. "That sounds amazing! I can't wait for our next adventure."

With promises of future outings, Nikki and Trish bid Amy goodnight and made their way into the house. As they settled down in the cozy living room, sipping hot mugs of tea, the warm ambiance and serenity enveloped them.

Nikki turned to Trish, gratitude shining in her eyes. "I'm so grateful to have moments like these, where we can come together as a family and create lasting memories. It's a reminder of the love and bond we share."

Trish reached for Nikki's hand, squeezing it gently. "I couldn't agree more. Today was not just about the farm or our parents' graves—it was about reconnecting as sisters, rekindling our relationship, and cherishing the moments we have together. I treasure our sisterhood, Nikki, and the moments we're building."

Nikki smiled, her heart swelling with affection for her sister. "Me too, Trish. Our journey today was filled with closure, connection, and the joy of finding new memories. I'm grateful for you and for our shared experiences."

As the evening unfolded, Nikki and Trish continued to reminisce about their day, sharing stories and laughing together. The walls of Trish's home reverberated with the warmth and love that had blossomed throughout the day at the farm.

As they finally retired to bed, their hearts were full of love, gratitude, and the knowledge their sisterhood would continue to thrive and grow, fortified by the precious memories they had created on that beautiful day at Kristofferson Farm.

Chapter Twenty-Six

Lacy

The pool deck buzzed with a frenetic energy as swimmers, coaches, and spectators bustled about. The smell of chlorine permeated the air, bringing back memories of countless swim meets from Lacy's past. She could feel a sense of excitement building within her as David prepared to compete, and she couldn't help but feel a surge of pride for her son.

Lacy glanced over at Phillip, who stood by her side, his eyes filled with warmth and encouragement. Over the past few weeks, they had been taking their relationship slow, getting to know each other on a deeper level. Lacy could see Maria's curiosity and fondness for Phillip growing, her daughter's playful attitude surfacing more and more each day. It warmed Lacy's heart to see the bond forming between them.

"Looks like a great turnout today," Phillip commented, his voice filled with genuine interest.

Lacy nodded, her eyes sweeping over the crowd. "Yes, it's always a busy event. Swim meets have a way of bringing people together."

As if on cue, Amy approached them with a mischievous grin. "Hey, Lacy! Ready to cheer on the star of the day?"

Lacy chuckled, delighted by Amy's infectious enthusiasm. "Absolutely! David is sure to give it his all."

From the corner of her eye, Lacy spotted David approaching, his swim cap pulled snugly over his short blond hair. He exuded a quiet confidence she hadn't seen in him in the past couple of months.

"Good luck, David!" Lacy called out, opening her arms for a quick hug. David obliged, a small smile gracing his lips.

Amy joined in the teasing, a playful glint in her eye. "Remember, David, don't forget to swim faster than your sister today!"

David rolled his eyes, but a hint of a smile tugged at the corners of his mouth. "I'll do my best, Amy."

Lacy, Phillip, Trish, Nikki, and Maria found their seats in the spectator area, their eyes fixed on the pool below. The sound of splashing water and echoing cheers filled the space as other swimmers dove into the water, competing in various events.

Trish leaned over to Lacy, a mischievous grin on her face. "I bet David's going to blow everyone out of the water. He takes after his aunt, you know."

Lacy laughed, playfully nudging Trish's side. "We'll see about that. Maybe he inherited some of my competitive spirit."

Their banter was interrupted by the sound of the announcer's voice booming through the loudspeakers. "Ladies and gentlemen, please direct your attention to the lanes for the next race, the 100-meter freestyle."

Nikki leaned forward; her eyes fixed on the starting blocks. "Do you see him, Lacy?"

Lacy squinted, scanning the row of swimmers lined up on the blocks. Finally, she spotted David, clad in his team's swim cap and goggles, poised and ready for the race.

"He's ready," Lacy said, her voice filled with pride.

As the race began, the pool erupted with a flurry of movement. David sliced through the water with precision and determination, his long limbs propelling him forward with each stroke. The crowd erupted into cheers and applause, their support washing over him like a wave of encouragement.

Lacy's heart swelled with pride as she watched her son race. The water gleamed as David powered through each lap, his focus unwavering. The noise of the crowd faded into the background as Lacy locked eyes with David, a silent message passing between them.

Finally, David touched the wall, his body heaving with exertion. The pool erupted into a roar of applause as he emerged from the water, a triumphant smile on his face.

Lacy, Trish, Nikki, Amy, and Maria rushed to the edge of the pool, cheering and clapping with unbridled enthusiasm. Their voices blended with the chorus of support surrounding them.

"You did amazing, David!" Lacy exclaimed as David approached them, his chest heaving with exhaustion.

David grinned, his eyes shining with a mixture of

pride and relief. "Thanks, Mom. I couldn't have done it without your support."

Lacy pulled him into a tight hug, her voice filled with emotion. "I'm so proud of you, David. You gave it your all out there."

As they basked in the afterglow of David's achievement, the bond between them grew stronger. Lacy couldn't help but feel a sense of gratitude for her family, their love and support emanating like a beacon of warmth in the winter air.

The rest of the meet passed in a blur of excitement and camaraderie. David's success had set the tone for the day, filling them all with a renewed sense of hope and joy. The rest of the meet was a whirlwind of activity with David winning his 200-meter freestyle, coming in second in the 100-meter backstroke, and his team securing the relay medley. But the crowning moment came when David was announced as the MVP swimmer of the competition. Lacy could hardly contain her excitement as she, Amy, Maria, Nikki, and Trish cheered loudly, their voices echoing around the pool complex.

"David, you were incredible!" Amy exclaimed, her eyes sparkling with excitement.

Maria chimed in, "You were like a fish, David! So fast!"

David chuckled, a flush of pride coloring his cheeks. "Thank you, everyone. I couldn't have done it without you all."

The group decided to celebrate David's victories with milkshakes at their favorite local spot. The air was crisp and cool as they walked down the street, their laughter and chatter filling the night.

Once they settled into a booth, Phillip turned to

David, "You were in top form today, David. Your dedication really paid off."

David nodded, his smile widening. "Thanks, Phillip. It felt good to swim well, especially with all of you there to support me."

As they sipped their milkshakes, conversation flowed easily among them, discussing the day's events, sharing jokes, and making plans for the future.

"I can't get over how well you did today, David," Nikki said, her eyes filled with admiration. "You've worked so hard and it paid off."

David blushed slightly, "I'm just glad I could make you all proud."

"Oh, you did more than that," Trish interjected. "You blew us all away. And that backstroke was a close one. Just a little more and you would have had it."

David nodded, "Yeah, I need to work on my flip turns. They're slowing me down."

Lacy watched the interaction with a warm smile, her heart swelling with pride and gratitude. She felt incredibly blessed to have such a supportive group around her and David.

As the day drew to a close, David announced his plans to head to the movies with his friends. Lacy, although a little worried, understood his need to celebrate with his peers.

"Make sure you drive safely, David," she admonished, her motherly instincts kicking in. "And call me when you get home."

"I will, Mom," David assured her, a grin on his face. He stood up, ready to leave, but not before giving Lacy a tight hug. "Thank you for everything."

Watching him leave, Lacy felt a sense of contentment

wash over her. Her family and newfound friends had shown her the true meaning of support and love, and for that, she was eternally grateful. As the night wrapped up, they all looked forward to their next adventure together, each of them carrying the joy and triumph of the day in their hearts.

After they returned home, Maria retired to her room to work on a school project. Phillip, having offered to help Lacy clean up, stayed back. The house was quiet, save for the soft clinking of dishes being put away and the occasional exchange of words between Lacy and Phillip.

Once they were done, Lacy decided to make hot chocolate, a staple in their household. Phillip watched as she moved about the kitchen with ease, her hands deftly preparing the steaming mugs. She handed one to him and took another up to Maria's room.

On her return, she smelled the familiar scent of hot chocolate filling the room.

"I've noticed you make hot chocolate a lot," Phillip commented, a playful smile tugging at the corners of his mouth.

Lacy laughed. "Yes, it's a bit of a family tradition. The kids love it, and so do I."

They settled into a comfortable silence, sipping their hot chocolate and letting the warmth spread through them. A movie played on the television, but Lacy found herself more interested in the man next to her, his presence comforting and familiar.

Halfway through the movie, Lacy realized she was leaning against Phillip, her head resting on his shoulder. She shifted slightly, preparing to sit up, but Phillip's arm wrapped around her, pulling her closer. She found herself curled up against his side, a sense of contentment washing over her as Phillip gently stroked her arm, eliciting goosebumps.

Phillip broke the silence, his voice low and warm. "I told my daughter about us."

Lacy turned to look at him, her heart skipping a beat. "Oh?"

He nodded. "She's studying abroad, but we're very close. She was thrilled to hear I've met someone special. She'd like to meet you."

Lacy laughed lightly, a hand coming up to cover her mouth. "Sounds like things are getting serious."

Phillip chuckled, his eyes softening as he looked at her. "Only if you'd like them to be."

Lacy's heart fluttered at his words, her mind whirling with thoughts. "I... I would very much like to meet your daughter, Phillip."

They spent the rest of the evening in comfortable companionship, sharing stories and laughter. As the night wore on, Lacy couldn't help but feel a sense of gratitude for the bond they were building. It was a simple, yet profound connection, one she hadn't expected but was immensely grateful for.

As the movie played on, Lacy and Phillip became more comfortable, their bodies relaxing against each other. Before long, the soothing rhythm of Phillip's heartbeat lulled Lacy into a peaceful sleep, her head resting gently on his chest.

Phillip, too, found himself drifting off, the warmth of Lacy's body against his and the serenity of the moment coaxing him into slumber. The movie continued to play on the television, its sounds becoming a distant hum as they both lost themselves in the tranquility of their shared comfort.

It was David's voice that broke the peaceful bubble. "Mom?"

Lacy stirred, her eyes fluttering open to find David standing over them, a cheeky grin on his face. "David," she mumbled, her voice thick with sleep. "What time is it?"

"Just after midnight," he replied, his grin widening. "I didn't mean to wake you up, but it's pretty late."

Phillip, roused by the conversation, woke up, a sheepish smile on his face as he sat up. "Did we really fall asleep?"

David chuckled, "Seems like it. Don't mind me though, you two can go back to your cuddling."

Lacy blushed, a soft giggle escaping her lips. "Oh, go to your room, you!"

David laughed, his eyes twinkling with mischief. "All right, all right. Goodnight, Mom. Goodnight, Phillip."

"Goodnight, David," they responded in unison, watching as David disappeared down the hallway.

Once David was gone, Phillip got up from the couch, stretching his arms. "I guess it's getting late," he said, his voice low. "I should probably head out."

Lacy, now fully awake, nodded. "Yeah, it is late. Thank you for staying, Phillip."

Phillip smiled at her, his eyes warm. "I enjoyed every minute of it, Lacy." He then leaned down, planting a gentle kiss on her cheek, causing her to blush.

"Goodnight, Lacy," he said, his voice barely above a whisper.

"Goodnight, Phillip," she replied, her heart fluttering as she watched him leave.

As Lacy settled back into the silence of her home, she

couldn't help but reflect on the unexpectedly wonderful evening she'd had. The bond she was forming with Phillip was something she hadn't anticipated, but she was grateful for it. As she drifted back to sleep, she found herself looking forward to their next adventure together.

Chapter Twenty-Seven

Lacy

L acy took a step back, her eyes scanning the beautifully decorated hall of the Nestled Inn. Fresh flower arrangements adorned every table, casting a floral scent that enhanced the cozy atmosphere. The soft glow from the fairy lights created a dreamlike ambiance, making Lacy's heart flutter with satisfaction.

Nikki, the bride-to-be, stood at the front of the room, her eyes sparkling with emotion. The guests settled into their seats, their excitement palpable. Lacy couldn't help but feel a wave of joy wash over her, blending with the sense of belonging that radiated from every corner of the room.

Nikki raised her glass, commanding the attention of everyone present. "Thank you all for joining us tonight," she began, her voice filled with warmth. "A year ago, I was living in my own little world, miles away from this town, hardly giving a second thought to the notion of family."

Her words hung in the air, and anticipation grew among the attentive guests.

"But then, tragedy struck," Nikki continued, her voice tinged with a mixture of sorrow and acceptance. "My sister, Trish, had an accident, and I found myself here in Camano, taking over her business and caring for her home."

The room fell into a reverent silence as Nikki's words resonated with her audience. Lacy's gaze lingered on her sister, grateful to see the depths of love and strength that had grown between them.

"In that moment," Nikki continued, her voice gaining strength, "this place, this town, it grew on me. It became my home. And from this newfound grounding, incredible things happened."

Lacy felt her breath catch as Nikki gestured toward her, a tender smile lighting up her face. "I connected with my sister, Lacy, and discovered a bond that had been lost to time. And then there's Amy," she said, her voice trembling with affection. "Trish's daughter, who has brought so much love and laughter back into our lives."

A wave of warmth surged through Lacy's chest as she caught Amy's eye, her niece's grin mirroring her own. They had found each other, filling a void that had long been ignored.

"And then," Nikki's voice quivered with excitement, "there's Paul."

As the name left her lips, the room seemed to hold its breath. All eyes turned to the man standing beside her, a mixture of anticipation and curiosity etched on the faces of their loved ones.

"Our love story," Nikki whispered, her voice teetering on the edge of tears, "it never died. Not even after all these years of separation."

Lacy watched in awe as Nikki and Paul locked eyes, their connection tangible, even from across the room. The depth of their affection needed no explanation. It was a flame that had weathered the storms of time, only to be rekindled with an uncontrollable fervor.

The room erupted in cheers, drowning out any doubt or hesitation that may have lingered. Lacy watched as her sister leaned down and pressed her lips against Paul's, sealing their love with a passion that could not be ignored.

All eyes turned to Sarah, the daughter of Paul, who smiled warmly at Nikki, her acceptance shining through.

The room erupted once more, applause and cheers thundering through the air. Lacy felt her heart swell with overwhelming happiness for her sister.

As she joined in the jubilation, Lacy couldn't help but feel an overwhelming sense of gratitude. In this moment, amidst the love and unity that surrounded them, she knew she was exactly where she was meant to be.

Nikki turned to Sarah, Paul's daughter, with a warm smile and a glint of gratitude in her eyes. "Sarah, thank you for being okay with me marrying your dad," she said sincerely. "I'm so grateful for your support, and I can't wait to officially become your stepmom."

Sarah returned Nikki's smile, her eyes reflecting genuine affection. "I'm happy for both of you, Nikki," she replied, her voice filled with warmth. "You make my dad really happy, and that's all that matters to me."

Nikki's heart swelled with gratitude as she turned to Paul, her eyes shining with love and anticipation. "Tomorrow, I get to marry my best friend and soulmate, and I can't wait," she said, her voice filled with emotion.

Paul's eyes met hers, and a soft, tender smile graced his lips. "I've been waiting for this moment for so long," he murmured, his voice filled with quiet intensity. "I can't wait to call you my wife."

As cheers erupted around them, Nikki felt a surge of joy and excitement. She leaned in, closing the distance between them, and pressed her lips to Paul's. The kiss was a sweet affirmation of their love, a promise of the future they were about to embark upon together.

The room filled with applause and happy exclamations as Nikki and Paul shared their intimate moment, the air buzzing with the palpable energy of love and anticipation. In that fleeting moment, surrounded by their loved ones, Nikki felt a profound sense of belonging and fulfillment, knowing she was about to embark on a new chapter of her life with the man she loved.

As they parted, Nikki and Paul exchanged a tender look, their eyes communicating volumes in the silent exchange. The promise of their future together hung in the air, a beacon of hope and love that illuminated the path ahead.

The evening continued with laughter, toasts, and heartfelt conversations, each moment etching itself into the collective memory of the night. It was a celebration of love, a testament to the enduring power of connection and the unwavering strength of the human heart. As the night unfolded, Nikki held on to the feeling of sheer joy and anticipation, knowing tomorrow would mark the beginning of a new and beautiful chapter in her life.

The morning of the wedding dawned with a soft, golden light filtering through the windows of the quaint inn. In Nikki's room, a buzz of excitement filled the air as Lacy, Trish, Amy, and Sarah gathered around Nikki, who sat in front of the mirror, her eyes sparkling with a mixture of nerves and joy.

Lacy carefully adjusted the delicate lace veil that adorned Nikki's radiant curls, while Trish fussed over the final touches of her makeup, her hands deft and gentle. Amy and Sarah stood by, their eyes shining with admiration and love for the bride-to-be.

"You look absolutely stunning, Nikki," Trish exclaimed, her voice filled with pride and affection as she stood back to admire her handiwork. "Paul won't know what hit him when he sees you walking down that aisle."

Nikki turned to look at her reflection, her eyes misting with emotion. "I can't believe this day is finally here," she whispered, her voice filled with wonder. "I'm so grateful to have all of you here with me."

The group of women enveloped Nikki in a warm embrace, the room filled with a chorus of affectionate murmurs and shared laughter. Lacy felt her heart swell with happiness as she witnessed the unbreakable bond between them, a tapestry of love and support that had carried them through both joyous and challenging times.

As the embrace broke, Trish fixed Nikki with a playful glare. "Now, remember, no tears," she teased, a mischievous glint in her eyes. "I worked hard on that makeup, and I won't have you ruining it with your sentimental nonsense."

Nikki chuckled, her eyes glistening with unshed tears. "I can't make any promises, Trish," she replied, her voice catching slightly. "It's just all so overwhelming."

Lacy sprang into action, reaching for a pack of blotting paper and deftly catching the tears before they had a chance to fall. "I've got you covered, Nikki," she said with a soft smile, her eyes reflecting the deep affection she felt for her sister. "No need to worry about a thing."

The room was filled with a tender warmth, a palpable sense of love and camaraderie that wrapped around them all like a comforting embrace. As they continued to prepare, the air buzzed with anticipation, each moment etching itself into the collective memory of the day.

In that room, amidst the flurry of final preparations, Lacy felt an overwhelming sense of contentment. She knew this day was not only about Nikki and Paul's love but also about the enduring strength of their family, a testament to the unwavering power of connection and the profound beauty of shared moments. As they readied themselves for the ceremony that lay ahead, Lacy held on to the feeling of sheer joy and gratitude, knowing she was about to witness a celebration of love that would linger in their hearts for years to come.

Lacy took a deep breath as she stood at the back of the lawn, admiring the beautifully arranged vintage setup for Nikki's wedding. Soft hues of pastel swept across the scene, like a page pulled from a forgotten fairy tale. The guests were buzzing with excitement, their eyes eagerly anticipating the grand entrance of the bride.

As Lacy walked down the aisle with her groomsman, her heart quickened its pace. She couldn't help but notice Phillip among the guests, his eyes locked on to hers, a smile dancing on his lips. The sight of him filled her with a joyous warmth, igniting a swarm of butterflies in the pit of her stomach.

Nikki's maid of honor, Trish, glided down the aisle, her presence commanding attention and admiration. Lacy's eyes lingered on her sister, her heart brimming with pride. Their journey had brought them here, standing side by side, celebrating love in its purest form.

Then, as if guided by a heavenly melody, the bride's marching song began to play. Time seemed to slow as Nikki emerged, appearing like an ethereal vision in her vintage dress, every detail carefully chosen to embody her romantic spirit. A collective gasp escaped the lips of the guests, their eyes drawn to her radiance.

Paul, waiting at the altar, couldn't conceal the tears welling in his eyes, overcome with emotion at the sight of his bride-to-be. He watched in awe as Nikki gracefully made her way down the aisle, her steps mirroring the elegance of a waltz. His love for her blossomed in that moment, brimming with a depth that words couldn't express.

As Nikki reached his side, their eyes locked, silently communicating everything the heart yearned to say. Lacy could practically feel the tangible connection between them, a love that had withstood the test of time and had emerged stronger than ever.

The celebrant's voice carried across the lawn, ushering in the beginning of the sacred ceremony. "Dearly beloved," the celebrant began, their voice carrying a sense of reverence, "we are gathered here today to witness the union of Paul and Nikki in holy matrimony."

Lacy's attention shifted between the bride and groom, eager to soak in every word, every glance that passed between them.

"Do you, Paul, take Nikki to be your lawfully wedded wife, to have and to hold from this day forward, for better or for worse, for richer or for poorer, in sickness and in health, as long as you both shall live?" the celebrant asked, their voice resounding with weight and significance.

Paul's voice trembled with raw emotion as he gazed at Nikki, his love shining through every word. "I do," he replied, a gentle smile gracing his lips. "With all my heart and soul, I do."

Nikki's voice, filled with a tender vulnerability, echoed her beloved's sentiment as she turned to him. "And do you, Nikki, take Paul to be your lawfully wedded husband, to have and to hold from this day forward, for better or for worse, for richer or for poorer, in sickness and in health, as long as you both shall live?"

Tears of joy welled in Nikki's eyes as she met Paul's unwavering gaze. "I do," she whispered, her voice carrying a universe of love. "With every fiber of my being, I do."

Lacy watched with an overwhelming sense of joy as the couple exchanged vows, their voices intertwining with a symphony of promises and devotion. The words echoed through the air, mingling with the gentle breeze that rustled the leaves overhead, bearing witness to the sacred union taking place.

As the ceremony unfolded, time seemed to stand still, each word and each gesture etching itself into Lacy's memory. Love, laughter, and shared dreams united in perfect harmony, filling the hearts of everyone present.

As the celebrant proclaimed them husband and wife, the air erupted in applause and jubilant cheers. Paul and Nikki sealed their union with a kiss, setting their collective future in motion.

Lacy stood amidst the joyous celebration, her heart overflowing with love for her sister and Paul, for the unbreakable connection that bound their families together. The vintage backdrop faded away, replaced by something far more precious—the enduring power of true love.

Chapter Twenty Eight

Lacy

The reception was in full swing, the vibrant energy of laughter and music filling the air. Lacy found herself pulled onto the dance floor by a beaming Phillip, his hand warm and reassuring in hers.

They swayed to the rhythm of the music, their steps in perfect sync, their gazes locked. A smile played on Phillip's lips as their dance took on a playful ease.

"Are you enjoying yourself, Lacy?" he asked, his voice filled with genuine curiosity.

A soft laugh escaped her lips as she looked up at him, her eyes shining. "More than I can put into words," she replied, her voice tinged with happiness, "and I'm dancing with the single most handsome guy at the wedding."

Phillip's eyes sparkled with warmth as his hand traveled to her temple, his touch tender against her skin.

"You're too kind," he replied, his voice barely above a whisper, "but I have something to confess."

Lacy's heart skipped a beat at his words, her curiosity getting the better of her. She tilted her head slightly, urging him to continue.

Phillip took a deep breath, his voice laden with vulnerability. "Lacy," he began, his voice almost a hushed secret, "I can no longer deny what I feel. I... I love you."

Lacy's breath hitched in her chest; her eyes wide with surprise. For a moment, time seemed to freeze as the weight of Phillip's words settled between them.

Pulling back slightly, searching his eyes for honesty, Lacy whispered, "Phillip... I'm falling in love with you too."

A rush of relief and adoration washed over Phillip's face, his smile radiant and genuine. "Oh, Lacy," he whispered, drawing her close, "I've never felt this way before—this depth of connection and love. You've become an integral part of my life, and I can't imagine it without you by my side."

Lacy's heart swelled with warmth and certainty as she looked into his eyes, knowing their heart's desires aligned. In that moment, she couldn't help but reflect on her own journey, the twists and turns that had led her to this point, where love seemed to dance before her in all its beauty and vulnerability.

As she watched her family and loved ones laugh and have fun, a sense of contentment settled over Lacy. The realization that this town had become her home, the place where love and belonging flourished, washed over her.

Nikki joined them on the dance floor, her eyes filled with joy as she witnessed the connection between Lacy and Phillip. "Lacy, my dear," Nikki whispered, her voice full of affection, "it warms my heart to see you so happy. Camano has grown on you, hasn't it?"

Lacy nodded, her smile widening. "It's more than that, Nikki," she confessed, her voice laced with certainty. "This town, this community, has become an integral part of who I am. I can't imagine leaving anytime soon."

Nikki embraced Lacy, a sense of shared understanding passing between them. "I'm so glad you've found your place here," she whispered, her voice filled with gratitude. "You've made our family whole again, Lacy, and for that, I will always be grateful."

As they swayed to the music, wrapped in a warm embrace, Lacy felt her heart bursting with love, hope, and an unwavering sense of purpose. In this moment, she knew she had found her own piece of happiness and a future filled with endless possibilities.

Coming Next

Pre Order Shadows of the Past

Other Books by Kimberly

The Archer Inn

An Oak Harbor Series

A Yuletide Creek Series

A Festive Christmas Series

A Cape Cod Series

Echoes of Camano Series

Connect

Connect with Kimberly Thomas

Amazon
Facebook
Newsletter
BookBub

To receive exclusive updates from Kimberly, please sign up to be on her Newsletter!

CLICK HERE TO SUBSCRIBE

Made in the USA
Middletown, DE
24 April 2025

74704974R00146